The Wonderful Dream

"Are you . . . saying," asked Claudia, "that . . . you love me?"

"I fell in love with you the moment I saw you," the Marquis replied. "And I intend to protect you."

"I . . . I do not . . . understand," Claudia murmured.

"What I am saying," the Marquis answered, "is that I will give you a house in St. John's Wood, or anywhere else you fancy, and I will be with you as often as it is possible."

Taking her hand in both of his, he said:

"You shall want for nothing, my lovely one, but I cannot offer you marriage . . ."

A Camfield Novel of Love
by Barbara Cartland

"Barbara Cartland's novels are all distinguished by their intelligence, good sense, and good nature. . . ."
—ROMANTIC TIMES

"Who could give better advice on how to keep your romance going strong than the world's most famous romance novelist, Barbara Cartland?"

Camfield Place,
Hatfield
Hertfordshire,
England

Dearest Reader,

Camfield Novels of Love mark a very exciting era of my books with Jove. They have already published nearly two hundred of my titles since they became my first publisher in America, and now all my original paperback romances in the future will be published exclusively by them.

As you already know, Camfield Place in Hertfordshire is my home, which originally existed in 1275, but was rebuilt in 1867 by the grandfather of Beatrix Potter.

It was here in this lovely house, with the best view in the county, that she wrote *The Tale of Peter Rabbit*. Mr. McGregor's garden is exactly as she described it. The door in the wall that the fat little rabbit could not squeeze underneath and the goldfish pool where the white cat sat twitching its tail are still there.

I had Camfield Place blessed when I came here in 1950 and was so happy with my husband until he died, and now with my children and grandchildren, that I know the atmosphere is filled with love and we have all been very lucky.

It is easy here to write of love and I know you will enjoy the Camfield Novels of Love. Their plots are definitely exciting and the covers very romantic. They come to you, like all my books, with love.

Bless you,

CAMFIELD NOVELS OF LOVE
by Barbara Cartland

A NEW CAMFIELD NOVEL OF LOVE BY

BARBARA CARTLAND

The Wonderful Dream

JOVE BOOKS, NEW YORK

THE WONDERFUL DREAM

A Jove Book / published by arrangement with
the author

PRINTING HISTORY
Jove edition / June 1994

All rights reserved.
Copyright © 1994 by Barbara Cartland.
Cover art copyright © 1994 by Fiord Forlag A/S.
This book may not be reproduced in whole
or in part, by mimeograph or any other means,
without permission. For information address:
The Berkley Publishing Group, 200 Madison Avenue,
New York, New York 10016.

ISBN: 0-515-11394-8

A JOVE BOOK®
Jove Books are published by The Berkley Publishing Group,
200 Madison Avenue, New York, New York 10016.
JOVE and the "J" design
are trademarks belonging to Jove Publications, Inc.

PRINTED IN THE UNITED STATES OF AMERICA

10 9 8 7 6 5 4 3 2 1

Author's Note

SEVILLE has been called "the one City in Spain that no visitor should miss."

There is something in the air of Seville which immediately communicates itself to every visitor.

It has been described as a sense of romance, of *joie de vivre*, a sense of colour and of life.

I found Seville fascinating, and as I was there just before Easter, I saw the famous procession start on Palm Sunday which continues until Easter Day.

Every balcony near the famous Cathedral was hung with palm branches and there were strange figures in every street.

There were penitents, ranging from small children to tall men, each carrying a lighted candle in the procession.

The statues themselves are fantastic. The *pasos*, which are all the Stations of the Cross, as well as the Madonna, were dressed in capes of satin or damask and glittered with precious jewels.

Spanish ladies empty their jewel caskets and shower the Virgin with gifts, and the *pasos*, mounted on platforms, are carried through the City by five or six dozen bearers.

They are so heavy that they have to stop every few yards to let their bearers have a rest.

Love is an all-important question in Seville, the City of Don Juan. He was actually called Miguel de Manara. He was rich, licentious, and careless of his life and wealth.

He has, however, remained in people's minds as a great lover.

But few people know that Miguel de Manara renounced his worldly goods and joined the Brotherhood of the Caridad.

It was their unsavoury task to collect the bodies of executed men and bury them.

It is perhaps this which has made the Andalusians, with their love of life, have a morbid preoccupation with death.

Everywhere in Seville one has little glimpses of what the Moors left behind.

The sunken garden pools and painted ceramic tiles make one remember that a great deal of the City's beauty comes not from the Spanish, but from those who at one time were their conquerors.

The Torre de Oro (Tower of Gold) was formerly linked to Alcazar by a subterranean passage because the Palaces of their Kings served as fortresses.

Catholic Monks added their own embellishments to where Sultans received their tributes of young virgins.

Charles V built a small Palace and a Hall where splendid tapestries depicted his triumphant expedition to Tunisia.

The gardens with their high walls covered with bougainvillaea are adorned with an Eastern Grotto, fountains, and in every patio there are high naked windows through which the Concubines peeped at their masters.

chapter one

1881

"WHAT shall I do?"

Claudia asked herself the question for the hundredth time, until it seemed to echo and re-echo in her ears.

"What shall I do?"

She had thought after her Father and Mother were burned to death, when the Theatre in which her Father was performing collapsed, that her whole world had come to an end.

Now, yet again, Fate had dealt her a terrible blow over which she had no control.

She had seen her Father and Mother off to the Theatre.

She had stayed at home, although it was the first night of *Hamlet*, because she had a cold.

"I will take you another night, Darling," her Mother promised.

She would never allow Claudia to go backstage in the Theatre.

Her Father was determined that neither she nor her Mother should have anything to do with the actors and actresses with whom he worked.

It always seemed to Claudia a little strange.

But because she was used to obeying Walter Wilton, as he was known professionally, she did not protest.

Her Mother explained when she was quite young that he wished to keep his life as an actor completely separate from that of being a husband and father.

"You see, Darling," she said gently, "your Father is famous in the Theatre and people make a great fuss of him. When he comes home, he just wants to be himself, and so we must do what he wants and look after him with love."

There was no doubt that was the care Walter Wilton received from his wife.

Claudia knew that her Mother waited every evening for the sound of horses' hoofs and wheels outside the door.

Then she would run eagerly down the stairs and be waiting for her husband as he came in.

He would close the door, take his wife in his arms, and kiss her possessively.

It was almost as if he had been half-afraid she would not be there when he returned.

Claudia used to think that no two people could be more happy together, or more in love.

They would sit hand-in-hand on the sofa, and they would talk to each other across the Dining-Room table in a manner which made every word seem a caress.

No girl, she thought, could have a more handsome Father or a more beautiful Mother.

Walter Wilton had been the son of the Headmaster of a large Boys' School.

He had, therefore, received an excellent education and had won a Scholarship to Cambridge.

There he had been one of the students who enjoyed acting.

During his time they had put on two Shakespearean Plays with Walter in the lead.

The students' parents and many other people came to watch them.

One night the owner of two Theatres in the West End of London had been in the audience.

He was impressed by Walter's amazing ability as an actor.

From that moment his future was assured.

He became, as the years passed, the most

important Shakespearean actor on the London Stage.

People flocked to see him, not only because his acting was so superb, but also because he was so handsome.

"He looks like a young Adonis!" women would say as they left the Theatre.

They would go back night after night to see him again.

Walter had the common sense to realise that his career as an actor did not assure him a place in Society, not even in his Father's world.

Anderson was Walter's real name and his Father explained rather uncomfortably to his son that he was not welcome at the School on Speech Day.

"They admire you across the footlights, dear boy," he had said, "but the parents do not wish their sons, and certainly not their daughters, to be mixed up with anyone who is an actor."

Walter had laughed, but he had felt somewhat humiliated.

Therefore, when he fell in love with Claudia's very beautiful Mother, he was determined that she should not be contaminated by the life he lived on the Stage.

Claudia had been sent to an expensive School in Kensington.

The Headmistress, however, had no idea that she was the daughter of Walter Wilton.

Claudia Anderson would certainly not have been accepted as a pupil had the Headmistress known.

Her Mother had explained to her how important it was that she should just be the daughter of two ordinary people.

She was warned never to speak of her Father to anyone, however friendly they became.

"It seems strange, Mama," Claudia said. "The other girls talk about their Fathers, but I can never mention mine."

"Just say he is often away from home," her Mother told her.

As she grew older, Claudia understood why she must be so secretive.

At the same time, it was impossible not to admire her Father and know that on the Stage he was breathtaking.

When he was speaking, the whole audience would sit in rapt silence.

Night after night he was applauded and brought back to take bow after bow before the curtain finally came down.

Then disaster had struck.

Walter Wilton was performing in one of the oldest Theatres in London; it was in the Drury Lane area.

After the fire had destroyed it, everyone said they should have realised in how dangerous a state the building was.

To lose her Father and her Mother in such

a terrible way was to Claudia like receiving a blow to her head.

It was impossible for her to think clearly.

She had been at home in the little house in Chelsea, nursing her cold, when she heard the news.

She was in the middle of preparing a drink of lemon and honey for her Mother, in case she should catch it too.

Someone hammered loudly at the door, and as there was no one else in the house, she opened it.

A man from the Theatre had been sent to tell her that her Father would not be returning.

He was almost incoherent because he too was so shocked by what had occurred.

The owner of the Theatre had managed to escape.

He had been kind enough to think that Walter Wilton's household must be told that he was dead.

What nobody had realised at the time was that Claudia's Mother was in the audience.

At first Claudia hoped against hope that her Mother had survived.

Finally, from the newspapers, she learned the truth.

The headlines were so flattering, she thought, that her Father would have been proud of them.

They read:

"WALTER WILTON DEAD."

"GREATEST ACTOR OF ALL TIME
KILLED WHEN THEATRE COLLAPSES."

"WALTER WILTON—
A LOSS TO ENGLAND AND THE WORLD."

"HOW COULD THIS HAPPEN
TO WALTER WILTON?"

She read them with Kitty, the daily maid who came in to clean the floors and brought the newspapers to her.

Kitty was crying because she had been very proud of her Master.

" 'Ow could it 'appen to 'im, of all people, Miss Claudia?" she asked. "It ain't fair 'e should 'ave been struck down like that!"

It was what Claudia felt herself.

She read those reports and others.

Apparently her Father had played the part of Hamlet more brilliantly than anyone had ever done it before.

He was going back to take his tenth curtain call.

The whole audience was cheering and shouting:

"Bravo! Bravo!"

Suddenly there was a crash, and the roofing

7

above the Stage had collapsed.

One of the beams had struck Walter Wilton on the head.

Then people were screaming as smoke came billowing out, not only from the back of the Stage, but also from one side of the Auditorium.

It was the side, Claudia was to learn later, on which her Mother had been sitting in one of the boxes.

She had been suffocated by the fumes before the fire got completely out of control.

Later her body had been found, burned almost beyond recognition.

Over fifty people lost their lives that night in the disaster. A great number of others had suffered severe burns and other injuries.

It had been a tragedy that had shocked the whole country.

Walter Wilton was buried with his wife.

Practically everybody from the Theatre world had attended the Funeral.

No-one took any notice of Claudia, who stood in the background.

She had been overwhelmed by the mountains of flowers that were placed on her Father's and Mother's graves.

She would have liked to thank all the people who had sent them.

But she knew that was something of which her Father and Mother would not approve.

It would have revealed what he had always kept secret—that he had a daughter.

Claudia had learnt from what she read in the newspapers that the Journalists were unaware until now that he had a wife.

When Walter was interviewed in his dressing room, he never talked about his private life.

Claudia found they merely referred to her Mother as "Janet Wilton."

They had little or nothing to say about her.

'It is what Papa would have wanted,' she thought.

But she could not help wondering what she herself should do.

The day after the Funeral she sat at her Father's desk and tried to discover what money he had.

She found his cheque-book, but she could not find any bank-statements.

When it was announced when the Funeral was to take place, she expected that a Solicitor would appear.

He would be able to tell her if her Father had made a Will.

It was something which had never struck her before as being necessary since her Father was still a comparatively young man.

Because he was so handsome and virile, it was impossible even to conceive the thought of his dying.

"He must have provided for Mama!" Claudia told herself.

She continued to go through the drawers, one after another.

She was sure she would find something which would be of help.

She had always known that her Father was over-generous towards those with whom he acted.

Her Mother had remonstrated with him over and over again.

"You have not given away all your money, Darling?" she would ask.

"Not all of it, my precious," her Father would reply. "But poor old Henry was in dire straits and I could not let him leave the Theatre empty-handed. I know he hasn't a chance of getting another part."

"That is his own fault," Claudia's Mother said. "After all, you told me yourself he was drunk on the night of your benefit. No manager is going to take a risk with one of his leading men behaving like that."

"I know, I know," Walter Wilton agreed. "At the same time, I feel sorry for him because he has not someone like you to look after him."

There was nothing her Mother could say after that, Claudia thought, except, as usual, to show her Father without words how much she adored him.

If "poor old Henry" needed money, there

were regularly a dozen other men like him.

And Claudia was sure that there were also women who cried on her Father's shoulder because they knew he would help them.

All actors depended on benefits, and Walter Wilton enjoyed them frequently.

But he would share the money he received with the other actors and actresses in the play.

"Your Father is always thinking of other people," Claudia's Mother said to her a dozen times, "and while I would not want him any different, it means that you and I have to scrimp and save."

Looking back, Claudia could not remember one moment in her life when her Father and Mother had not been supremely happy.

The house, small though it was, seemed to be filled with love.

When Walter Wilton was not working, they would go and stay in the country in some small but comfortable Inn.

They would walk over the fields and play *"Hide and Seek"* with her in the woods.

Her Mother would tell her stories of the fairies and goblins who lurked there.

It was they who became Claudia's companions.

It was only when she was older that she thought it rather strange that while they had a very comfortable little home, there were never any visitors.

The only occasions when her Father had people come to see him was when they came from the Theatre to discuss a new part for him.

Invariably she and her Mother would sit in the bedroom until they had left.

"Why can we not meet Papa's visitors?" Claudia had asked when she was still quite young.

"Because your Father wishes to keep us all to himself," her Mother answered, "and when you are older you will understand."

Claudia had got older, but she had not understood.

She had still thought it strange.

Her Father, as he grew more and more famous, was asked to a great number of parties to which he never took her Mother.

"Do you not mind staying at home, Mama?" Claudia had asked once.

"No, Darling, and that is the truth," her Mother replied. "Your Father keeps the two worlds in which he moves apart, and I am perfectly content with the one which consists of just you and me."

There was no doubt her Mother was speaking the truth.

At the same time, Claudia, when she left School, thought a little wistfully that she would like to go to some of the parties at which her Father was the Guest of Honour.

They were not only theatrical parties.

In fact, they were often given by Lords, Earls, Marquesses, and Dukes.

Claudia then discovered that the aristocrats who entertained her Father did not have their wives at the parties they gave for him.

Instead, there were attractive actresses from other Theatres.

Claudia found that few of the girls who became her friends at School had ever been allowed to visit the Theatres in the West End.

They were occasionally taken to an Opera or concert if it was considered suitable for them.

Even the Plays of Shakespeare were banned as being too sensational for a girl who would be in a few years a Social *débutante*.

After the Funeral, Claudia, sitting alone at home, realised she had no real friends.

When she was at School she had been out once or twice to tea with girls with whom she was friendly.

Her Mother, however, had not encouraged her to accept such invitations because she could not ask them back.

"Why not, Mama? Why can they not come here when Papa is performing at a Matinée?"

"Because if they did, Dearest, someone would learn sooner or later that Walter Wilton is your Father. In which case you would no longer be able to attend the School."

"How could anybody think Papa was like those ignorant actors I hear you talking about?" Claudia asked indignantly.

"It is difficult to explain," her Mother replied, "but the Stage and Society do not mix. Therefore, my Darling, you must refuse that invitation you have just received from Lady Letchmore's daughter and say that your Father and Mother are taking you to the country on that day."

Grudgingly because she wanted to go to the party, Claudia did as she was told.

When she was alone she realised that not only had she lost her Father and Mother, but the whole world that had been hers since she was a child had come to an end.

"What am I to do . . . what am I to do?" she asked.

* * *

Later that afternoon Claudia heard a knock on the front-door.

Kitty had gone home before luncheon.

Claudia was still searching through her Father's desk.

She had run to the front-door wondering who it could be.

When she opened it she was astonished to find outside a very smart man-servant.

Beyond him was a carriage drawn by two

horses, with a coachman, wearing a cocked top-hat, holding the reins.

When she appeared, the footman, without saying anything, went down the steps to open the door of the carriage.

A very elegant, elderly Lady, wearing a hat festooned with feathers, stepped out.

She walked slowly to where Claudia was standing.

Then she asked:

"Are you Claudia?"

A little belatedly, because she was so surprised, Claudia dropped a small curtsy.

"Yes, Ma'am," she replied as her Mother had taught her to do, "that is my name."

"I am your Godmother," the Lady said, and walked past her into the house.

It was a second or two before Claudia could collect her wits.

Then she showed her into the small Sitting-Room which opened out of the narrow hall.

She thought afterwards that it would have been better to have taken her upstairs to the Drawing-Room, which was on the First Floor.

But for the moment it was difficult to think of anything but how smart the Lady looked.

It seemed impossible that she had a Godmother of whom she had never heard.

The small room was very comfortably furnished, but Claudia thought that her visitor was inspecting it critically.

Then she said:

"Let me look at you, child."

Claudia stood in front of her and asked as she did so:

"Are you . . . really my Godmother? I . . . I never . . . knew I had . . . one."

The Lady laughed.

"I suppose I should not be surprised that you have not been told. In fact I am Lady Bressley, and I held you in my arms when you were baptised."

As she finished speaking, Lady Bressley sat down in an armchair.

"You are very like your Mother," she said. "She was one of the most beautiful people I have ever known!"

"You have . . . heard what . . . happened to her?" Claudia asked hesitatingly.

"I read the newspapers," Lady Bressley replied, "and that is how I found you. One of them actually gave the address of this house."

That must have been a newspaper she had not read herself, Claudia thought.

She wondered if other people would come and call on her.

Then Lady Bressley asked:

"What are you going to do now that your Mother is dead?"

"I . . . I do not . . . know," Claudia replied. "I have been going through my Father's papers, trying to find out if there is any money. But although I have found his cheque-book, there does not seem to be any statement from the Bank."

"That does not surprise me," Lady Bressley said. "Although Walter Wilton must have earned a great deal, I doubt whether, like all his kind, he ever saved a penny."

There was a scathing note in Lady Bressley's voice, which Claudia resented.

She thought, however, it would be a mistake to say anything in her Father's defence.

"Are you alone here?" Lady Bressley asked.

"Yes, I am," Claudia answered, "and it is very frightening being without Mama and Papa."

"I can understand that," Lady Bressley said, "and I suppose, as I am your Godmother, that you are now my responsibility!"

Claudia looked at her wide-eyed as she went on:

"We have a great deal to decide, but the first thing is whether or not you should approach your Father."

"B-but . . . I thought you knew . . . Papa is . . . dead too! He was . . . killed at the Theatre."

"I am talking about your *real* father," Lady Bressley said, "not Walter Wilton!"

"I . . . I do not . . . know what you are . . . saying!" Claudia protested. "He *was* my . . . Father!"

Lady Bressley shook her head.

"No, my Dear, and now that you are eighteen, it is time you learned the truth."

"The . . . truth?" Claudia murmured.

"It seems incredible that your Mother has never told you, but I suppose I can understand that she did not want you to feel embarrassed, as you would have been."

"About . . . what?" Claudia questioned. "I . . . do not . . . know what you are . . . talking about."

"Then let me explain," Lady Bressley said. "Your Mother was the daughter of the Earl of Porthcarian. She was married when she was the same age as you to Viscount Niven, who has now come into the title and is the Earl of Strathniven."

Claudia gasped.

She did not speak, and Lady Bressley went on:

"Your Mother behaved very badly by running away with Walter Wilton after they had met in Edinburgh, when he was giving a performance there at the Theatre. So I think it unlikely that your Father would be in a hurry to welcome you to his Castle."

"I . . . cannot believe . . . what you are . . . s-saying!" Claudia said piteously. "H-how is it possible that . . . P-Papa is not . . . my Father? I . . . I loved him!"

"I am sure you did," Lady Bressley said

18

in a kindly tone. "He was a very handsome man and, as I have always heard, more or less a Gentleman. But he could not marry your Mother because she was already married!"

"And . . . she actually . . . ran away with him?" Claudia asked, her voice sounding strange even to herself.

"You were one year old at the time," Lady Bressley said. "When your real Father was away from home on a shooting-party, she packed her bags and, taking you with her, left Scotland for England with an actor, who was not so well known in those days, called Walter Wilton."

Claudia gave a little gasp.

"This is . . . extraordinary!"

"I can understand your feeling like that," Lady Bressley said gently, "but as I have said, child, it is time you learnt the truth and started to think about the future."

"B-but . . . why did you . . . never come to . . . see Mama?" Claudia asked.

"I tried to find out her address," Lady Bressley explained, "but she had cut herself off from her family and everyone she knew. I thought then that perhaps I would not be welcomed, but merely looked upon as if I were interfering. Was she happy—really happy— with the man she ran away with?"

"I cannot imagine that any two people could have been happier!" Claudia said. "They loved each other . . . and also . . . they loved me."

She thought as she spoke that she had never imagined for a moment that Walter Wilton was not her real Father.

She was certain he had loved her.

No man, she thought, however well he acted, could have pretended the kindness, the understanding, and the affection he showed her.

"Well, I am glad of that!" Lady Bressley was saying. "Janet was always my favourite ever since she was a tiny child, and in a way I can understand why she fell in love with anyone so handsome as Walter Wilton."

"Wh-what is the . . . man you say is my . . . F-Father . . . like?" Claudia asked falteringly.

"He is a rather strange man, and was twenty years older than your Mother. I think he loved her in his own way," Lady Bressley said, "but he is very reserved and your Mother must have felt trapped in his large, dark Castle."

"It was . . . very brave of . . . her to run away," Claudia remarked.

"Very brave indeed!" Lady Bressley agreed. "And not only was her husband furious, but also your Mother's Father. He raged, he talked of shooting the actor who had stolen his daughter! But in the end he did nothing except, of course, to cut your Mother out of his Will and say that never again was her name to be mentioned in his presence."

"I wish Mama had . . . told me all this," Claudia whispered.

"I think that might have been insulting to the man she loved," Lady Bressley said slowly.

Claudia knew she was right.

It was far happier for all of them for her to believe that Walter Wilton was her real Father.

He had in fact accepted her as if she had been his own child.

"Now that you have learnt the truth," Lady Bressley said, "we have to decide what you shall do."

Claudia said nothing, and after a moment she went on:

"There is no hurry. It would be best to give your Father time to learn that your Mother is dead, and perhaps make enquiries as to what has happened to you."

"Perhaps, after all these years, he will not be interested," Claudia suggested.

"That is a distinct possibility," Lady Bressley agreed. "So while we are giving him time to think, I suggest you come with me."

Claudia's eyes lit up.

"Do you . . . mean that? . . . Do you really . . . mean it?"

"Of course I mean it," Lady Bressley said sharply. "You can hardly stay alone here in this empty house with no-one to chaperon you, and with, I imagine, very little money."

"I am sure there must be some," Claudia said apologetically, "and I was intending to call at Coutts Bank and . . . ask them to tell me what is in my F—Walter Wilton's account."

She struggled over the name as she was just about to say "my Father's."

"My Secretary can see to that for you," Lady Bressley said. "What you have to do now is to pack your clothes, and I will provide you with some more because we are going abroad."

"Abroad?" Claudia exclaimed.

"I have already arranged to visit Spain, where I have friends," Lady Bressley explained, "and I will take you with me."

Claudia clasped her hands together.

"To Spain? I would love to go to Spain! Mama and I read some books about it, and I learnt a little, a very little, Spanish at School."

"Well, that, at any rate, will be helpful," Lady Bressley said. "But we will have a Courier with us, so all we have to do is to leave it in his capable hands and enjoy the journey."

"I cannot . . . believe . . . it!" Claudia exclaimed.

Suddenly she was very near to tears.

Impulsively, she moved forward to kneel at Lady Bressley's feet.

"It has been . . . very frightening . . . wondering what I should do . . . and where I should go . . . and now you have come magically . . . as if out of the sky . . . and every-thing has changed."

Lady Bressley put out her hand to touch Claudia's cheek.

"You do not have to worry any more, dear child," she said. "I have been a lonely old woman since my husband died seven years ago. I have had companion after companion who always bored me and I got rid of them. It will be delightful to have you with me."

"Oh, thank you, thank you!" Claudia cried. "I only hope that I can be of use and do things for you so that you will never regret asking me."

"I loved your Mother," Lady Bressley said, "and you were a very pretty baby. I feel sure we have a great deal in common."

"I hope so," Claudia said.

"You are a very sweet girl," Lady Bressley said, and kissed her.

Looking back, Claudia thought at that moment, when she least expected it, the sun had broken through the darkness.

She was no longer alone.

Instead, she was being transported to a magical new world.

How could she have known, how could she have guessed, that there was another shock to come, just as disastrous and almost as terrible as the first one had been?

chapter two

"RUN upstairs, my Dear," Lady Bressley said, "and get ready to come back with me to my house. I will send servants to pack your clothes so that you need not trouble to do anything yourself."

Claudia had done as she was told.

She changed from the simple dress she was wearing into her best gown, which her Mother had bought for her a few months before.

Only then did she wonder what would happen to the house.

She went into her Mother's bedroom and was instantly aware of the fragrance that she had made essentially her own.

It was the scent of white violets, and Claudia

thought it would always haunt her.

Her Mother's clothes were all hanging tidily in the wardrobe.

She went to the dressing-table and took out the velvet box in which her Mother had kept her jewellery.

There were not many jewels.

But whenever Walter Wilton had any money to spare, he spent it on something which he knew would delight his wife, something that would, as he had said, reflect the stars in her eyes.

"I must not leave this behind," Claudia told herself.

She did not search for money, knowing there was none.

All that she could find had already been spent on the Funeral.

Claudia had given the Undertakers Walter Wilton's gold watch to compensate for the lack of gold sovereigns.

They had accepted it reluctantly.

When she went downstairs, her Godmother was sitting where she had left her.

She looked up as Claudia came into the room.

"You look very smart, my Dear," she said, "but then, your Mother always had good taste."

"I am afraid," Claudia said, "I have . . . not many clothes at . . . the moment. Mama was

26

waiting for the benefit from *Macbeth* to buy me two new gowns."

"I will buy you anything you need," Lady Bressley answered, "but we will have to do so in a hurry because you must do me credit in Spain, especially as my taking you with me will be a surprise."

"It is so . . . very kind of . . . you," Claudia said, "but I am just . . . wondering what I should do . . . about the house."

"My Secretary, Mr. Prior, will see to that," Lady Bressley answered, "and we will make a decision when you return as to whether you wish to sell it or keep it. It is always a mistake to do things in a hurry."

They drove off in the carriage with its fine horses.

Claudia felt as if she were living in a dream. She only hoped she would not awaken too soon.

Lady Bressley's house in Grosvenor Square was very impressive.

There seemed to Claudia to be an army of servants to look after them.

During the next few days Dressmakers seemed to come to the house every hour.

She had expected to have to go to the shops to buy her clothes, but Lady Bressley was so important that they were only too willing to come to her.

Evening gowns, day gowns, coats, jackets,

hats, all were brought for her approval.

For the first time in her life, Claudia found how tiring it was to be always fitting on clothes.

They left for Spain, travelling by carriage to Tilbury, from where they were to board an Ocean Liner.

Claudia was astonished at the number of people who went ahead of them.

There was a Courier to see to the luggage, and two footmen to carry it.

Then there was Lady Bressley's lady's-maid and a Secretary, who was to see that their accommodation on board ship was exactly to his employer's requirements.

In addition, there was, to her surprise, a coachman.

"I intend to hire a carriage and good horses when we reach Spain," Lady Bressley explained, "and I have no intention of being driven by someone I do not trust. Hopkins has been with me only a year, but he is an excellent driver."

It all seemed to Claudia very luxurious.

She realised when they stepped aboard the Ocean Liner that Lady Bressley was treated as if she were Royalty.

"I have travelled a great deal since I have been a widow," she told Claudia, "and the Chairman of this Line is a personal friend. He always gives orders that I am to be looked after properly."

Their accommodation was certainly the best on board.

An adjoining cabin had been converted into a Sitting-Room, because the Liner did not have Suites.

There were two Stewards constantly in attendance.

The food, Claudia learnt, was specially prepared for them by the Chefs.

As she lay in her extremely comfortable cabin, she said a prayer of thankfulness every night that she had been so fortunate.

It was during the days when they were choosing her clothes that Lady Bressley talked to her about her future.

"Perhaps, dear child," she said, "when we get back, you will want to meet your Father. But for the moment I think it would be a mistake to write to him."

"Why?" Claudia enquired.

"Because he will have seen in the newspapers that Walter Wilton is dead and that your Mother died with him. We must give him time to consider whether he should get in touch with you—before you approach him."

"I . . . I understand," Claudia said, "And I think . . . that is . . . sensible."

"You will, therefore," Lady Bressley went on, "call yourself Claudia 'Coventry,' which was my Surname before I married, and only when we come back to England will you use your title."

Claudia looked startled and her Godmother said with a smile:

"You must realise that, since your Father is now the Earl of Strathniven, you are Lady Claudia Niven."

Claudia gave a little gasp.

"But of course," Lady Bressley went on, "we have to remember that from a social point of view, your Mother burnt her boats, and the scandal in Scotland when she ran away with an actor still remains in the minds of some of the older people."

"I suppose ... they were ... all very shocked," Claudia said in a low voice.

"*Horrified* would be a better word!" Lady Bressley answered. "But, as I have already said, my Dear, I do understand, because your Mother's marriage was arranged by her Father in collusion with the then Earl of Strathniven."

She paused for a moment before she said:

"The two old Gentlemen put their heads together and thought of what was good for their Clans. The feelings of their respective children hardly came into it."

"And my Father ... my *real* Father ... was very much older ... than my Mother?"

"He was nearly forty," Lady Bressley said, "and is now, of course, approaching his sixtieth year."

Claudia thought of how handsome Walter Wilton had been.

He had also been young enough to laugh with her Mother.

Sometimes, when they teased each other, they would seem like two children.

She hesitated before she asked another question:

"Should I . . . not be wearing . . . mourning for . . . Mama?"

"Certainly not!" Lady Bressley said. "It is important that no-one in London connects you in any way with the death of Walter Wilton, and you will of course never mention him to any of my friends."

She spoke sharply.

Because Claudia had been so fond of the man she had believed to be her Father, she was loyal enough to say:

"He was always . . . very kind to me."

"I am sure he was, Dear," Lady Bressley replied, "but because he was also intelligent, he would understand that I am doing what is right for you when I say that you must forget him."

She paused for a moment before she went on:

"When we get back from Spain I intend to introduce you to the Social World, and as my Godchild you will be accepted in the highest and most important circles."

She spoke in a tone of satisfaction.

Then she said seriously:

"But, remember, Claudia, if it is known that you were living in Walter Wilton's house, then you will be ostracised by everybody, just as your Mother was."

Claudia wanted to say that it had not worried her Mother in the slightest, but she knew it would be a mistake.

Instead, she kept silent, and Lady Bressley continued:

"My friends in Spain will accept you without question as my Goddaughter. When we return, as I have said, you will decide whether to claim your position as your Father's daughter."

There was no question of Claudia arguing about it.

She told herself that she must remember that her name was Claudia Coventry.

She was aware that the servants in Grosvenor Square had addressed her as that.

It was also on the door of her cabin.

As they entered the Bay of Biscay, Claudia felt she had left her old world behind and was sailing into a new one.

It was not only very different, but also very exciting.

Her Godmother's lady's-maid looked after her.

For the first time in her life she had her bath prepared for her, her clothes pressed, and her hair arranged.

Certainly the attention to her hair transformed her appearance.

She thought when she looked at herself in the mirror that it was hard to recognise little Claudia Anderson, a girl who had no friends except the few she had made at School.

She had been aware of one thing, however.

Because she lived with Walter Wilton, she was very much better read and more advanced in her education than they were.

He had taken a First Class Degree at Cambridge and was extremely intelligent.

He had helped her with her homework.

He also made her help him when he was learning his lines.

"You speak beautifully," Lady Bressley said to her, "and when you read to me I feel that your voice is like music!"

With difficulty Claudia did not say that it was all due to the man she had thought was her Father.

She knew that it annoyed Lady Bressley when she mentioned him.

She therefore said nothing.

The sea was rough as they passed across the Bay of Biscay, and Lady Bressley stayed in bed.

Claudia was not allowed out of the Suite.

"If you break a leg or an arm, which is easily done in a very rough sea," Lady Bressley said, "it will be very tiresome, and nobody wants an invalid as a guest."

"I can understand that," Claudia agreed, "and I will be very careful."

After they had steamed past the Bay of Biscay, at last Claudia was able to explore the decks and look at the other passengers.

The majority of them were sailing to India.

The rest were leaving the ship at various ports on the way.

Quite a number disembarked at Lisbon, and the next port of call was Cadiz, where they themselves left the ship.

Owing to the excellent organisation of Lady Bressley's Secretary, a comfortable carriage drawn by two well-bred horses was waiting for them on the Quay.

Hopkins, whom she had not seen since they left London, immediately took charge.

As soon as their luggage was piled on the back they set off with the Courier and the lady's-maid sitting on the box.

Lady Bressley and Claudia travelled alone inside the carriage.

They had disembarked at Cadiz early in the morning.

They had then driven some distance before reaching a large Inn, where they were to stay the night.

It was a Posting-Inn very much the same as those in England.

Claudia knew that the horses would be changed there, so that they would have a fresh pair to carry them to-morrow.

She thought the Posting-Inn was quite comfortable.

Lady Bressley, however, disparaged it and said it in no way compared with the ones she had found in France.

Everything was done for her comfort.

She had brought her own sheets and pillow-cases with her.

Her maid, Emily, had packed every little accessory to which she was accustomed.

Claudia was entranced by the countryside through which they were passing.

The undulating land, with glimpses of mountains in the distance, was attractive.

The rivers and the picturesque villages kept her staring out of the windows. She was afraid of missing something.

It was therefore a relief when Lady Bressley dozed off and she did not have to follow a conversation.

They left the Inn after breakfast early the next morning.

The weather was good and they made excellent progress before luncheon, which they had brought with them.

They ate it by the side of a stream which glistened in the sunshine.

It was all very lovely.

Claudia kept thinking how lucky she was to be seeing Spain and hearing the Spaniards speak their language.

She had been delighted to find at the Inn that she could understand some of what was being said.

At the first opportunity, she thought, she would buy a dictionary.

Then she could learn every new word she heard which she did not understand.

It was growing very hot as the afternoon progressed.

Claudia was soon hoping that it would not be long before they reached their destination.

She knew they would spend their last night at another Hotel before reaching Seville.

The road narrowed and there were high rocks on either side of it.

The horses, although they were getting tired, were travelling at a good speed.

Suddenly, from round a corner, there came towards them a huge wagon drawn by four horses that appeared to be out of control.

It crashed into them.

The horses screamed, men shouted, and the wheels of the two vehicles clashed together.

The carriage containing Lady Bressley and Claudia overturned.

Badly shaken and dazed, Claudia was only vaguely aware of what was going on, and of being conveyed to the Hotel at which they had intended to stay.

There she was treated by a Doctor for slight concussion.

Still dazed, she was helped into bed by a kindly Chambermaid and given something to help her to sleep.

Only when the night was past and morning dawned did she learn the full extent of the tragedy.

Lady Bressley had been killed instantly.

The Courier had a broken leg, the coachman a badly cut face.

By what seemed a miracle, she and the lady's-maid had escaped with only a few cuts and bruises.

Three of the horses had had to be destroyed, and the carriage was incapable of going any farther.

The local Priest called to see her.

He suggested that Lady Bressley should be buried in the local Church-yard.

The Courier had already stated that it would be difficult to convey her body back to England.

Claudia had no idea what her family would wish done.

As she did not know any of them, she agreed.

It was the Courier, even though he could not move, who arranged everything.

Claudia and the lady's-maid were the only mourners as the coffin was lowered into the ground that afternoon.

When they arrived back at the Hotel, Claudia asked to see the Courier.

He was taken in a wheel-chair to one of the Reception Rooms.

"I want to return to England!" she said to him.

"I can make arrangements for you to go as soon as you wish, Miss Coventry," the Courier replied, "but the Doctor insists that I must not leave here for at least two weeks."

He gave her a sharp look before he said:

"I can afford it with the money Madam gave me for the journey."

Claudia did not say anything.

When she was alone in her room, she realized that she had no money.

The only thing she would be able to offer the Hotel to pay for her room and meals was her mother's jewellery.

She still felt limp and upset by what had happened, which was not surprising.

She felt she could not at the moment face the uncomfortable performance of explaining her predicament to the Proprietor.

It would be even more difficult if he did not speak English while her Spanish was very limited.

'I will do it to-morrow,' she decided.

She then went straight to bed without going down to dinner because her head ached.

* * *

When Claudia awoke next morning, she could think more clearly and told herself she had been very silly.

Of course there was money—not her own—but her Godmother's, which she carried in a despatch-case.

Claudia knew she kept it in her bedroom in the charge of her lady's-maid.

Lady Bressley would certainly not have come abroad without plenty of money both for the journey and for all other needs during her visit.

'How could I have been so stupid as not to think of that?' Claudia thought.

She also knew that Lady Bressley had carried jewellery with her.

She always wore a considerable amount, and Claudia wondered if it had been placed for safety in the Hotel safe.

Both the cases had been beside her in the carriage.

She would also wear a bracelet and make-up even when she was in bed.

"There will be plenty of money to pay for my ticket back to England," Claudia told herself.

She had not yet been called, but she got out of bed.

Pulling back the curtains, she rang the bell

for Emily, who should have called her some time ago.

As Emily had been almost unharmed in the accident, she would have collected the two cases.

She would have kept them safely in her room, or in the Hotel safe, while Lady Bressley was being buried.

"It was very foolish of me not to think of it before," Claudia chided herself, "but they will be perfectly safe with Emily."

Because she was impatient, she rang the bell again.

One of the Chambermaids opened the door:

"You ring, *Señorita*?" she asked.

Slowly, because she had to think out every word, Claudia asked her to fetch Lady Bressley's lady's-maid.

The Chambermaid understood and disappeared.

She came back about a quarter-of-an-hour later to say:

"Maid go away, *Señorita*, she leave."

Claudia looked at her in astonishment.

"I think there is some mistake," she said.

The maid did not understand.

Claudia began to dress, and when she went downstairs she asked for the Courier.

He had been accommodated on the Ground Floor because of his injuries.

After what seemed a long time, a Porter

wheeled him into the Reception Room, where Claudia was waiting for him.

"I am sorry," she said, "to have to send for you, but I have just been informed, though I am sure it cannot be true, that Emily has left. What can have happened? Where can she have gone?"

The Courier paused for a moment before he replied:

"I am afraid this will be a shock, Miss Coventry, but she has indeed left with Hopkins, who I thought was a trustworthy man."

"But . . . why? Have they . . . returned to . . . England?"

"I understand from the Proprietor that last night they asked for Her Ladyship's jewellery which had been placed in his care by those who carried you to the Hotel after the accident. He said they also asked for the case which contained, I think, Her Ladyship's money, and certainly the papers and the return tickets which I had given into her keeping."

"Are you . . . are you . . . saying," Claudia asked, "that . . . they have . . . stolen everything?"

"They have indeed! I am afraid, Miss Coventry, you are going to find yourself in a very uncomfortable position."

Claudia stared at him.

It was hard to believe that what he said was true.

If it was, then she was completely penniless, except for her Mother's jewellery which, without realising it, she had clung to even after she was injured.

She had carried it with her when she left Cadiz because Lady Bressley had said that sometimes the luggage was stolen off the back of a carriage.

It would be taken off without the passengers usually being aware of it.

Claudia had felt that she could not bear to lose the things her Mother had prized.

They were all she owned now, except for the contents of the house.

She was glad she had followed Lady Bressley's example by carrying them with her.

It seemed incredible that Emily should have suddenly become a thief.

Or that Hopkins, of whom Lady Bressley had spoken so highly, should have decamped with everything that was valuable.

She wondered if she should send for the Police.

As if he could read her thoughts, the Courier said:

"The Spanish Police will not show any interest, as we are foreigners. The best thing you can do, Miss Coventry, is to get back to England as quickly as you can."

He spoke in a somewhat disagreeable voice.

Claudia knew instinctively that he had no wish to be responsible for her.

Now that his rich Patron was no longer available, he was concerned only with his own problems.

She went back to her room to stare blindly at the expensive clothes which her Godmother had bought for her.

She felt it was farcical that she should be so well dressed and yet have no money.

She opened the box which contained her Mother's jewellery.

Compared with Lady Bressley's, it made a very poor show.

There was a diamond brooch, but the diamonds were very small.

There were pearl ear-rings which her Mother had loved, but the pearls were by no means perfect, nor particularly valuable.

There was an attractive coral necklace, but coral was not expensive.

There was a bracelet with a number of charms on it which Walter Wilton had given her Mother. It was certainly very attractive, and Claudia had loved it ever since she had been a child.

She had been almost as thrilled as her Mother was each time a new charm had been added to it.

But she thought a Jeweller would pay very

little money for it, and it would break her heart to part with it.

The rings might be worth rather more.

One ring contained three diamonds and Claudia had always believed it was her Mother's engagement-ring.

Otherwise there was nothing except for several very pretty but unsaleable pairs of ear-rings.

They matched the bead necklaces her Mother wore in the Summer.

Claudia knew that other pieces Walter Wilton had given her Mother had been sold to pay for her own education.

At other times, when things had been difficult between Shows and Walter had needed a new suit, something had been sold to pay for it.

She looked carefully at the contents of the jewel-box.

She wondered if there would be enough, even if she sold everything, to pay for the cheapest accommodation aboard a ship.

There was the sound of voices, and she realised it was after one o'clock and time for luncheon.

She therefore carried her jewel-box with her and went slowly down the stairs.

After luncheon, she thought, she would talk to the Proprietor.

He would be busy now, and it would be

wisest to acquaint him with her predicament when the meal was over.

But when she sat down at the table she found herself too shocked and worried to eat more than a very little.

Neither did she feel fit, after all, to face the Proprietor.

Going back to her bedroom, she lay down miserably on her bed, and mercifully fell fast asleep from sheer mental and emotional exhaustion.

It was late in the afternoon before she awoke.

Feeling much better and now even hungry, she dressed for dinner and went down to the Dining-Room.

She was aware that new people were coming into the Dining-Room who had not been there before.

There was a man and a woman with three children who were all making a great noise.

There was a man alone whom she could not help noticing because he appeared to be English.

He was tall, broad-shouldered, and, she thought, very distinguished-looking.

He was obviously of importance.

The Proprietor himself bowed him to the best table in the Dining-Room.

It was near a window which opened onto the garden.

Two waiters were told to attend to him,

while the wine-waiter hurried quickly to his side.

'I am sure he is English,' Claudia thought. 'I wonder if he would help me?'

Then she knew she would be far too embarrassed to approach anyone who appeared to be so grand.

More people came into the room to occupy the empty tables.

But the tall Englishman was receiving far more attention than anybody else.

Like her, the rest of the people in the Dining-Room were kept waiting until his needs had been catered to.

At last, the Englishman had given his order.

A bottle of wine was brought to his table for his approval.

He took one sip and sent it away.

Although she was worried for herself, Claudia could not help being amused.

She felt that if any ordinary person had taken that attitude, there would have been an argument.

The Proprietor would undoubtedly have protested that the wine was the best he could provide.

Without there appearing to be any difficulty about it, however, another bottle was fetched by the wine-waiter.

It was shown to the Gentleman and uncorked.

A little was poured into a wine-glass, which he tasted.

There was an almost audible sigh of relief as he nodded his head.

The glass was filled and the bottle put into the ice-cooler.

While all this was happening, Claudia was aware that the waiter who had been attending to her was nowhere to be seen.

She knew she would have a long wait for the next course.

As she sat waiting patiently, all she could do was to worry about talking to the Proprietor.

She found it impossible, however, not to watch the Gentleman.

He was now being tempted with delicious dishes which had not been offered to any of the other guests.

He was certainly very particular.

There was also a disdainful look about him.

Claudia thought it impressed the waiters, who were used to their aristocrats being haughty.

Then, as if the way she was looking at the Gentleman somehow attracted his attention, he looked across at her.

Their eyes met.

They were directly facing each other, as it happened, with no-one in between.

Claudia had the feeling that he was surprised by her appearance.

She had no idea that among the dark and somewhat swarthy Spaniards, she looked like someone from another Planet.

The blue of the gown which Lady Bressley had bought for her from Bond Street accentuated the gold of her hair and the translucence of her skin.

Her large eyes seemed to fill her small, pointed face.

It was from her Mother that Claudia had inherited her long, dark eye-lashes.

They curled back like a child's and the tips of them were touched with gold.

Because she was suddenly aware that she was staring at the Englishman, as he was staring at her, Claudia lowered her eyes.

She was looking down, yet was perceptively aware that the Englishman was still looking at her.

'He must think it strange that I am alone,' she told herself.

It was something that had not struck her before.

Now she was aware that it was very reprehensible for a young girl of her age to be staying in a Hotel unchaperoned.

'The sooner I go back to England, the better,' she thought as she finished her dinner and left the Dining-Room.

As she did so, she was careful to avoid looking towards the Englishman again.

Back in her bedroom, once again she was faced with the problem of how she was to travel with no ticket and no money to pay for it.

'I shall have to sell Mama's jewellery,' she thought despairingly.

There was nothing else, unless she offered her services and worked in the Hotel.

The thought flashed through her mind, but she knew at once how impractical it was.

"I have to think this out sensibly," she told herself, "just as Papa . . . I mean . . . Walter Wilton would have told me to do."

She felt as if he were beside her, saying:

"Use your brain—think only of the important things in life. Think! Do not do anything on an impulse, but weigh up every possibility before you act."

He would often talk to her like that.

She wondered now if he had been preparing her for the day when she would learn that she was not his child, and would have to decide her own future.

But even Walter Wilton, clever as he was, could not have anticipated the terrible situation in which she would find herself.

First, when he and her Mother were killed.

Now, when she was alone in Spain with no-one to help her, and no money.

chapter three

SUDDENLY there was a knock on the door.

"*Entrar*," Claudia said.

The Chambermaid who had looked after her before appeared.

"*El Señor* wish speak with *Señorita*," she said.

She opened the door wider, as if to indicate that Claudia should go with her.

She thought it must be the Proprietor who wished to speak to her about her plans and to learn how long she would be staying.

She knew it was going to be an awkward interview when she informed him that she had no money.

She would have to explain that Emily and

Hopkins had taken everything with them.

At least it would give her an opportunity to ask the Proprietor if anything could be done about catching them.

But she had the uncomfortable feeling that he would not be interested.

All he would want was to be paid for what she owed, and that meant sacrificing her Mother's jewellery.

She walked across the room to where the maid was waiting.

"Take me to the *Señor*," she said in Spanish.

The Chambermaid hurried along the passage and, still on the First Floor, stopped at a door.

Claudia had expected that she would be taken down to the Proprietor's office.

She had assumed it was on the Ground Floor near the main Entrance Hall.

The maid was knocking, however, on a door, and someone said:

"Come in!"

She opened the door and Claudia walked ahead.

She found herself in a small Sitting-Room which was somewhat over-furnished.

To her astonishment, she saw, standing in front of the fireplace, the Englishman whom she had noticed in the Dining-Room.

"Good-evening, Miss Coventry," he said.

"Allow me to introduce myself. I am the Marquis of Datchford, and as you also are English, I wanted to talk to you."

"I noticed . . . you in the . . . Dining-Room," Claudia said.

The Englishman looked so handsome and so over-powering that he made her feel shy.

"And I noticed you," he said. "Will you sit down?"

It flashed through Claudia's mind that perhaps he had been told of her predicament and would help her to get back to England.

If that was true, she would be very, very grateful.

She sat down on the end of the sofa and put her hands in her lap.

Her face, as she looked up at him, was like a child's in the presence of a School-Master.

"First," the Marquis said, "let me commiserate with you on the terrible accident in which you were involved. I have been told that the Lady with whom you were travelling was killed."

"It was . . . very frightening," Claudia said in a low voice, "and I . . . suppose I am . . . lucky to be . . . alive."

"Very lucky," the Marquis agreed. "I have also been told that the servants who were accompanying you have absconded with the Lady's jewels and money."

"That is . . . true," Claudia said. "Unfortunately I was struck on . . . the head when the accident . . . happened, and I hardly realised what had occurred. Otherwise I suppose I would have . . . asked for Lady Bressley's jewels to be . . . put in the . . . safe."

"You can hardly blame yourself," the Marquis said. "The servants have certainly behaved in a most disgraceful manner!"

He paused for a moment before he said:

"In England we would have sent for the Police, but I am sure things are very different in Spain."

"That is what . . . I thought," Claudia agreed, "or I would have . . . asked the Proprietor to . . . notify the Police."

"I do not think he would be very keen to do so," the Marquis said. "It would cast aspersions on the Hotel. People would not wish to stay here if they might be robbed."

"I . . . I did not . . . think of . . . that," Claudia answered, "but . . . of course . . . you are right."

There was a short silence before the Marquis said:

"I imagine, in the circumstances, that you are in an uncomfortable position."

He spoke as if he were choosing his words, and Claudia said frankly:

"To be honest, My Lord, I am wondering how I can pay the bill. As I have no money of

of the Opera House, sang two songs.

Then, with a great deal of bowing and curtsying, the guests left.

Those who were staying in the Palace were ready to go to bed.

There were three elderly ladies who, Claudia gathered, chaperoned the Princess and also acted as her Ladies-in-Waiting.

There were several close friends of the Prince's who were about the same age as he was.

When Claudia went to her own bedroom she thought that the poor girl must have a very dull life.

There were many visitors to the Palace but they were all very old.

So she was not surprised that Princess Louisa had kissed her affectionately good-night.

She said she was looking forward to to-morrow.

In her bedroom a maid was waiting to undo her gown.

When she got into bed, the woman told her that she would be called at eight o'clock in the morning.

She then extinguished the lights, except for those beside the bed.

When she was alone, Claudia looked up at the ceiling, with its painting of Venus surrounded by Cupids.

'I have never been in such a grand room as

this before,' she thought, 'and it is something I must remember.'

It was then she heard a knock on the communicating door between her room and the Marquis's.

Before she could answer it, he came in.

He was wearing a long, dark robe which reached to the ground. It was frogged, giving him a military appearance.

As he walked across the room towards her, she looked at him wide-eyed.

When he reached the bed he said:

"I came to say good-night, and also to tell you how splendidly you behaved to-night. I want you to know how grateful I am for such an outstanding performance."

"I was . . . afraid I might . . . do something wrong," Claudia said.

"No, you were perfect!" the Marquis assured her. "And what did you think of your first Royal party?"

Claudia gave him a little smile.

"I was very impressed. However, I could not help feeling that if you had to do that night after night, year after year, you would soon find it very dull."

"You are quite right," the Marquis agreed, "I would find it excruciatingly boring."

"Princess Louisa is a very nice girl," Claudia remarked.

"As a friend, I agree with you," the Marquis

answered. "As my wife—no!"

The way he spoke was so emphatic that Claudia laughed and said:

"You are quite safe now."

"Thanks to you," the Marquis replied. "But you do realise that we have to be very, very careful not to make anyone suspicious."

"You must tell me what I have to do," Claudia answered.

"I had intended to do that to-morrow," the Marquis said, "but first let me say again how grateful to you I am for not having put a foot wrong."

He sounded so relieved that Claudia thought it was almost insulting.

Then she remembered that he had no idea that her Mother would have taught her how to behave as a Lady.

He did not know she had been to a School where almost every pupil was the daughter of an aristocrat.

"We need not, in the circumstances, stay any longer than we have to," the Marquis was saying. "But as I came to see the Prince's horses, I cannot appear to be in too much of a hurry to leave."

"I hope he will be impressed by the ones you were driving," Claudia said.

"He will see them to-morrow," the Marquis replied, "but I suspect what he really wants is that I should admire *his* stables."

"I do hope that I shall be able to come with you," Claudia said. "I love horses!"

The Marquis raised his eye-brows.

"You can ride?" he asked.

"Yes, I can ride," Claudia answered, "but I have never been able to do so as often as I would have liked."

She thought how she had always ridden when her Mother and Walter Wilton had taken her to the country.

They had all ridden then.

Walter Wilton, having ridden as a boy, was in fact a very good horseman.

But her Mother had been exceptional.

She had therefore insisted that Claudia should have riding lessons whenever they could afford it.

It was not so much that she needed lessons, but that this gave her horses to ride, and the instructors would take her and other pupils into the Park.

Wistfully Claudia said now:

"What I would like, although I know it is impossible, is to ride some really fine horses on the land over which we drove on our way here."

"It might be arranged," the Marquis said, "but I doubt it."

He did not seem particularly interested, and Claudia said quickly:

"I must not be greedy. You have given me

the moon. I must not ask for the stars as well."

The Marquis laughed.

"I am glad you are satisfied. You certainly have an impressive room in which to sleep."

"It was intended to be yours," Claudia said, "but I hope the one to which you have been relegated is comfortable."

The Marquis did not speak for a moment.

He seemed to hesitate.

Claudia suddenly had the frightening thought that perhaps there was no bed in the dressing-room.

Then he said:

"I think you will understand, Claudia, as we are supposed to be on our honeymoon, that it would look strange if I slept in the dressing-room and the servants were aware that only one side of this bed had been slept on."

Claudia looked at him in sheer astonishment.

As if he realised that what he had said shocked her, he said quickly:

"What I am going to suggest is that I lie down for a short while on the other side of the bed. It will look in the morning as if it has been occupied, although of course, as I promised you, I will return to my own room to sleep."

"Oh . . . I understand," Claudia said. "Of course it is . . . very clever . . . of you to . . . think of that!"

"I thought you would agree," the Marquis answered.

He went round to the other side of the bed, pulled back the bed-clothes, and crumpled the top sheet.

He then lay down on the top of the bed with his head on the pillow.

Claudia watched him wide-eyed.

"I have always believed," the Marquis said, "that if you are going to tell a lie, it must be a good one. No doubt the Prince is disappointed that there is no question now of my becoming his son-in-law."

"I thought . . . he was a . . . little upset," Claudia said.

"I think it was Fate, or perhaps just my good luck, that you appeared at exactly the right moment to save me."

As the Marquis spoke, he got off the bed, giving the pillow a punch where his head had lain.

He then walked across to the communicating door.

"Good-night, Claudia," he said. "Sleep well and to-morrow you must not forget that I am relying on you."

"As I am . . . relying on . . . you," Claudia repeated.

"You can always do that," the Marquis answered.

He reached the door and smiled at her before

he went into his own room.

Claudia blew out the candles.

In the darkness she said to herself:

"He is very, very much nicer than I expected he would be, and he no longer frightens me."

She paused, wondering if her Mother and Walter were watching over her.

Then she added:

"Wherever you are, Mama and Walter, I hope you can see me now and how grand I have suddenly become! It will not last, but for the moment it is very exciting!"

chapter five

CLAUDIA found, to her disappointment, that after breakfast the Prince took the Marquis off to see his horses and she was not invited to go with them.

She found, however, when Princess Louisa joined her that she had arranged to take her into the City.

Claudia was eager to see the sights of Seville, as she had read so much about them.

Yet it would not be the same as being with the Marquis and seeing the Prince's horses.

Princess Louisa had now accepted her as a friend.

She talked quite intimately of herself and her family.

"I want to be married," she said, "and as quickly as possible. In fact, I had hoped, as Papa did, that the Marquis could be my husband."

"But surely," Claudia questioned, "you do not want to have an arranged marriage?"

The Princess looked at her in surprise.

"All our marriages are arranged," she said, "and only when I am married will I be free."

She realised Claudia was looking puzzled and explained:

"At the moment, I have these Ladies-in-Waiting with me always. They listen to everything I say and never stop telling me what I must not do."

She paused for a moment before she went on:

"You must be aware that it was only by making a scene that I have been allowed to drive alone with you to-day. Even so, two of them are following behind us in another carriage."

"I agree it must be tiresome," Claudia said sympathetically.

"It is far worse than that," the Princess groaned. "I can never be alone with a man or talk to him without their being present."

"And to be sometimes unsupervised is, I suppose, what you want," Claudia said.

"Of course I do," the Princess agreed. "Now

I am going to let you in on a secret—I have been meeting one of Papa's *Aides-de-Camp* and it is very exciting!"

"Will that not get you into trouble?" Claudia asked tentatively.

"Papa would be furious if he found out, and the *Aide-de-Camp* would certainly be dismissed. But we meet in secret places, and when he kisses me it is wonderful!"

Claudia looked at her in amazement.

"You have let one of the *Aides-de-Camp* kiss you?" she asked. "Surely that is very wrong?"

"Spaniards have passionate natures," the Princess explained, "and I do not really think that an Englishman would suit me. But Papa knew the Marquis is very important, and of course, he has wonderful horses."

Claudia thought for a moment. Then she said:

"I have always understood that Spanish Royalty are very particular about who their daughters marry. I would have expected your Father to choose a Royal Prince for you."

The Princess laughed.

"He tried to find one, but it was very difficult. He then discovered, which pleased him very much, that your husband's Great-Great-Grandmother was a Princess of Leichenburg."

"So that makes him a suitable match for a

Princess!" Claudia remarked.

She was really thinking it out for herself, but the Princess replied:

"Of course it does! I only hope the Marquis is very loving, and exactly what you want in a man."

Claudia thought she could not answer this, and the Princess went on:

"While Englishmen are known to be cold and reserved, Spaniards and Italians are very passionate."

Claudia thought it extraordinary that the Princess, who was so young, should know this.

She thought it would be a mistake to encourage her in her love-affair with the *Aide-de-Camp*.

She was sure it would get them into deep trouble if they were found out.

The carriage drove down a wide avenue and past a huge fountain to the Cathedral.

It was certainly breathtaking.

Claudia had read that it was the greatest Gothic building in the world.

She could see that the rich decorations and the great works of art were unique.

Inside, the Cathedral was so enormous that it was impossible for her eyes to take it in all at once.

The Princess showed her the precious relics of St. Ferdinand, then the glorious Mausoleum of Christopher Columbus.

Claudia discovered she knew far more than the Princess did about the great explorer.

Bitterly disillusioned by failure to find a Western route to Asia, he was first buried at Santo Domingo, then at Havana.

His body was brought to Seville, Claudia explained, only after Spain had lost all suzerainty over the New World he had discovered.

"I did not know that," the Princess said. "Poor Christopher Columbus! If he knew about it, he would have been very disappointed."

Claudia was looking at the huge Mausoleum.

She was thinking that in a way every man was a Christopher Columbus, exploring, trying to find something special, often, like Columbus, to be defeated at the end.

It made her feel sad, and she was glad when they went back to the Palace for luncheon.

There was no sign of the Prince and the Marquis.

After luncheon it was too hot to go outside.

Instead, they sat in the shade on the balcony, while Princess Louisa talked incessantly about herself.

When at last the Marquis returned, Claudia was thrilled to see him.

"Have you had an educational day?" the Marquis asked a little mockingly.

99

"I took your wife to the Cathedral," the Princess said before Claudia could speak, "but the story of Christopher Columbus made her sad. She thinks all men are explorers in their own way, but most of them become disillusioned sooner or later, just as poor Columbus did."

The Marquis raised his eye-brows.

"Do you really think that?" he asked Claudia.

"I have read about the lives of many great men," she answered, "and most of them never achieved their objectives. Or else gained and then lost them, which made things worse."

"I can see you are a cynic!" the Marquis observed. "Of course I am trying in every way possible, now that I have found you, not to lose you."

Claudia thought he was speaking for the benefit of the Princess, who was listening.

"I hope you will never do that!" she quickly replied.

When they went up to dress for dinner, she learnt there was to be another party to-night.

It, too, was being given for the Marquis's benefit.

"Of course, if I had known you were bringing your young and very beautiful wife," the Prince remarked, "I would have arranged for there to be dancing. As it is, I believe you will enjoy a game of chance, so my guests to-night are mainly men who like gambling."

After dinner the guests, and there were twenty of them, moved into the *Salon*.

A Roulette table had been set up, and there were also tables arranged for games of cards.

Claudia did not go with them.

She was alone in the *Salon*, where they had gathered for dinner, when the Prince came to her side.

"You are not a gambler, Marchioness?" he asked.

Claudia shook her head.

"I would always be afraid I might lose, so I would also not really enjoy it if I won."

The Prince laughed.

"That is a very sensible way to view gambling, in which I always think the odds are against the gambler."

"That is what my Father used to say," Claudia replied without thinking.

She realised she had been automatically referring to Walter Wilton.

Then she was afraid the Prince would ask her questions about her family.

She therefore said quickly:

"I cannot tell Your Royal Highness how much I admire your wonderful pictures. I never imagined I would see so many masterpieces all in one place!"

"My daughter has shown you the Picture

101

Gallery?" the Prince asked.

"Not yet," Claudia answered.

"That is an omission which must be rectified immediately," the Prince said. "Come with me!"

They walked from the *Salon* and along one of the wide, impressive corridors.

There were fine pictures hanging on either side of it, alternating with exquisitely carved mirrors that reached almost to the ceiling.

There were statues which Claudia wanted to examine.

But the Prince moved on until they climbed a wide staircase which opened onto one end of the Picture Gallery.

It stretched for a long way.

Claudia thought it would take them hours to inspect every picture, if that was what the Prince intended.

He showed her first *Las Meninas*, which was one of Velázquez's greatest works of art.

Claudia thought the small girls in their large crinolined dresses were enchanting.

She also loved the big dog lying beside them.

The Prince was pleased at her appreciation.

He was also surprised to find that she knew a considerable amount about the artists themselves and realised she was not just trying to please him by being enthusiastic.

He went past several pictures, then stopped

before one that Claudia had never seen in reproduction.

"This," he said, "is *The Naked Maja*, one of Goya's most famous paintings."

Claudia knew it was stupid of her.

Yet somehow she felt shy to be looking at a completely naked young woman.

She was lying back against soft pillows with her hands behind her head.

To her astonishment, the Prince said in a deep voice:

"That is how I would like to see you!"

For a moment Claudia thought she could not have heard him aright.

Then, as she blushed and would have turned away, his arms went round her.

"You are very lovely," he said, "so lovely that you make my heart beat faster, and I want to kiss your lips which look so innocent and strangely untouched."

It was not only what he said, it was the note in his voice and the fire which she saw in his eyes that frightened Claudia.

She did not scream, but she began to struggle against him.

Relentlessly he drew her closer.

She turned her head frantically from side to side, but his arms seemed like bands of steel.

She knew it was only a question of time before he captured her lips.

Then, just as she knew despairingly how

ineffectual she was against his strength, a voice said from the far end of the Gallery:

"Ah, there you are, Claudia! I wondered where you had got to."

The Prince's arms relaxed, and Claudia fought herself free.

Then she was running wildly and as swiftly as she could towards the Marquis.

Only as she reached him did she slow down.

She was just about to throw herself against him in relief that he had saved her, when he said in a cold, commanding voice:

"The Princess is looking for you. You will find her in the *Salon*."

The way he spoke drew Claudia abruptly to a halt.

Her arms were outstretched towards him, her eyes turned to his.

He deliberately walked away from her towards the Prince.

She could not believe it was happening.

Then he said loudly in a lofty tone:

"Your Royal Highness has a magnificent Gallery, and I believe I am right in saying that your collection is recognised as one of the finest in the world."

As he was speaking, he had moved away from Claudia.

She realised he was pretending not to have noticed anything amiss.

She was still frightened, however, and her

heart was pounding in her breast.

She ran down the stairs, and back along the corridor.

She told herself she could not face the other members of the party, nor, for that matter, the Princess.

When she reached the hall, she went up the main staircase to her bedroom.

It was too early for the maid to be waiting for her.

She sat down on the stool in front of the dressing-table and tried to control her breathing.

Her heart was still beating tumultuously.

She had never been so frightened as when the Prince had pulled her against him and attempted to kiss her.

Then, as she began to breathe more easily, she told herself she was being very foolish.

The Princess was kissed by one of the *Aides-de-Camp*.

Why should she feel upset if the Prince wished to kiss her?

Yet she had never imagined that a man to whom she had hardly spoken, and who was so very much older than she was, would behave in such an extraordinary fashion.

"I am sure it is because he is Spanish," she told herself. "An Englishman would never behave in such a disgraceful manner."

Then she realised that she knew nothing

about Englishmen either, having met so few.

She thought of the compliments she had received last night and to-night from the Gentlemen sitting next to her at dinner.

She had believed it was merely because they were Spanish and thought it was no more than good manners to flirt with a married woman.

If they had known she was a young, unmarried girl, they would undoubtedly have ignored her.

"It was stupid of me to be frightened," she said. "I might have known from Princess Louisa that men expect a married woman to be sophisticated and, as far as they are concerned, fair game!"

She was certain, however, that Walter, because he loved her Mother, would never have behaved like that.

She could not imagine her Mother allowing any other man to kiss her, or to be in any way familiar.

'The Prince had no right to take me to see a picture of a naked woman!' she thought indignantly.

Suddenly she felt very young, very foolish, and very vulnerable.

What did she know about the world in which she found herself?

What did she know of anything?

She had lived in a little house in Chelsea, spending many hours a day at School.

The girls she met there had all been as innocent as she was herself.

She was certain that none of them had been kissed, since they were all strictly chaperoned.

They were taken to and from School by their Governesses, who resided in their homes.

'I wish Mama had told me more about the world before she died,' she thought sadly. 'Perhaps now that I am grown up . . . other men will . . . behave . . . like the . . . Prince.'

She shivered at the thought.

She did not like to think what might have happened if the Marquis had not arrived at exactly the right moment.

Later, she rang the bell.

One of the maids came to help her undress, and she got into bed.

She did not blow out the candles.

She felt sure the Marquis would come to tell her what had happened after she left.

She lay thinking of how beautiful the room was.

But its owner was an unpleasant old man who should not thrust himself upon his guests, however important he might be.

It was over two hours later before she heard the Marquis go into the room next door.

She could just hear him talking to his Valet.

Then there was the sound of the door onto the corridor closing.

A minute or two later the communicating

door opened, and the Marquis came into the bedroom.

Claudia sat up in bed.

As he came across the room towards her she could see his face in the candlelight.

She realised he was very angry.

He reached the bed and demanded furiously:

"What the devil did you think you were doing going to the Picture Gallery alone with the Prince?"

"He offered . . . to show me his pictures," Claudia answered.

"And you were gullible enough to go with him, without taking anybody else with you! How could you do anything so idiotic?"

"I . . . I did not expect . . . any man to . . . behave like that," Claudia stammered.

"Of course any man would behave like that if you encouraged them by going alone! Good Heavens! You must have enough common sense to know that was an invitation to him to make love to you!"

"H-how . . . was I to . . . know . . . that?" Claudia asked piteously. "I n-never imagined anyone as . . . old as the Prince would . . . want to . . . k-kiss me!"

"Then you must be half-witted!" the Marquis stormed. "Of course any man would want to kiss you, looking as you do! You should not have put yourself in such a position, which made it very uncomfortable for me."

"It was . . . uncomfortable for m-me!" Claudia protested. "He . . . frightened me!"

"Of course he frightened you, if you really had no idea that was what he intended to do."

"Do you really think if I had suspected he would . . . behave in that horrible manner I . . . would have . . . gone there with him?" Claudia asked. "We were talking about pictures and he said he would show me the Picture Gallery because the Princess had failed to do so. How could I . . . refuse?"

The Marquis sat down on the side of the bed.

He was looking at her, then, quite unexpectedly, he smiled.

"It was my fault, Claudia," he said. "I ought to have warned you, but thinking of you as Walter Wilton's daughter, it never occurred to me that anyone could be so innocent and quite so ignorant of the world as it is."

"I . . . I told you I would . . . m-make mistakes," Claudia said miserably.

"You have made none until now," the Marquis said, "and I believe the Prince thought I was unaware of what had happened. I talked quite normally about his pictures before we finally left the Gallery."

"P-perhaps I should . . . go away," Claudia said in a low voice.

"We will do that the day after to-morrow," the Marquis replied, "and you will be quite safe until then, since the Prince is taking me into the country to-morrow to see his race-horses. We shall be away all day, and I will arrange for us to leave the following morning."

"And . . . you will take . . . me back to . . . England with you?" Claudia begged.

There was a pleading tone in her voice and in her eyes.

The Marquis looked at her for a moment before he said:

"Of course I will take you with me. I was not intending to talk about your future until we reached England, but now, as you are so upset, I want you to listen to me."

"I . . . I am listening," Claudia said.

"Because you are so young and unspoiled," the Marquis said slowly, "what happened to-night will happen to you again wherever you go."

"Oh, no! No!" Claudia cried. "I could not . . . bear it!"

"I am afraid it is the penalty for being so beautiful. And you *are* beautiful, Claudia— the most beautiful person I have ever seen."

Because no-one had ever spoken to her in that way before, Claudia stared at him in astonishment.

"What I am going to suggest to you," he continued, "which I was going to keep until we reached England, is that you will allow me to protect and look after you."

Claudia's eyes widened.

"Are . . . are you . . . saying," she said after a moment, "that . . . you love me?"

"I fell in love with you the moment I saw you in the Dining-Room of the Hotel," the Marquis replied, "and last night, when I came to lie down on the bed, it was very difficult to keep my promise not to frighten you, and to leave you alone."

He drew in his breath before he said:

"And I intend to do the same to-night, as I do not want to rush you, or upset you in any way. But when we get to England, I must protect you from other men."

"I . . . I do not . . . understand," Claudia murmured.

"What I am saying," the Marquis answered, "is that I will give you a house in St. John's Wood, or anywhere else you fancy, and I will be with you as often as it is possible. At least two or three times in the year we will be able to go abroad together on my yacht."

He spoke very tenderly.

Yet, as he finished, he knew that Claudia still did not understand.

Taking her hand in both of his, he said:

"You shall want for nothing. You shall have horses, jewels, servants, anything you require, my lovely one, but I cannot offer you marriage.

You must try to understand that it would be utterly and completely impossible for me in my position as head of a noble family."

"You . . . mean," Claudia said in a voice he could hardly hear, "because . . . I am the . . . daughter of . . . Walter Wilton?"

The Marquis did not answer, and after a moment she said:

"D-does that . . . matter so much when you . . . s-say you . . . love me?"

She felt the Marquis's hand tighten on hers before he replied:

"I want you! God knows I want you, but I am tied by my blood, by tradition, by the generations that have gone before and will come after me. I know it is difficult for you to understand, but I cannot hurt those who look up to me, and I cannot demean the name that has been part of English history all down the centuries."

He was choosing his words very carefully. Then he said in a different tone:

"If you are on your own, I do not like to think what will happen to you. There will be men— of course there will be men—dozens of them— wanting you, pursuing you, all behaving as the Prince behaved to-night."

Claudia made a little murmur of horror, and the Marquis went on:

"That is the choice you have to make, my Darling, between being alone and fighting by yourself, or allowing me to protect and keep you safe. I will also love you in the way you should be loved."

There was silence before he added:

"I am not going to try to persuade you, because I do not want to frighten you. I am going to leave you to make the decision for yourself, and you can give me your answer when we go home the day after to-morrow."

He rose from the bed.

Then, as he was still holding her hand, he raised it to his lips.

Very gently he kissed it.

Then, unexpectedly, he turned her hand over and kissed the palm passionately and possessively.

It was something Claudia had not imagined happening.

She felt a strange thrill run through her.

Then, as the Marquis raised his head to look at her, she saw the same fire in his eyes that there had been in the Prince's.

Something within herself responded to it.

For a moment he just stood, looking down at her.

Then, as if he could not help himself, he bent towards her and kissed her.

His lips were gentle and yet possessive.

Then with what was an effort he stood up.

"Good-night, my lovely one!" he said. "Dream of me as I shall dream of you."

Before Claudia could speak or even think, he walked across the room to the communicating door.

As he reached it he turned back, and just stood looking at her.

Then he left, closing the door quietly behind him.

chapter six

WHEN the Marquis had gone, Claudia stared into the empty space where he had stood.

It was as if she could not believe he was no longer there.

It was then it swept over her like a flood tide that she loved him.

She had loved him ever since he had driven her away from the Hotel, but had not realised it was love.

Then suddenly she realised that his reasoning for being unable to marry her was based on misinformation.

She was not Walter Wilton's daughter!

As soon as she told him the truth, everything would be changed.

The thought made her thrill with excitement.

She jumped out of bed and started to run across the room just as she was, in her nightgown.

Then, as she reached the closed door, she was suddenly still.

He had said he could not marry her although he loved her.

But really he did not want to be married at all.

If she told him who she really was and that her Father was the Earl of Strathniven, he might feel trapped.

He would feel the same as when he realised he was being manoeuvered into marrying Princess Louisa.

"But I must tell him . . . I must!" her heart urged her.

At the same time, her brain told her that she would be putting him in a very difficult position.

Then, just as if the whole situation became clarified, she knew all too surely that he did not really love her.

Her Mother had loved Walter Wilton overwhelmingly.

She had given up her husband's title and her own. She had gone into exile because of her love.

She had been well aware of the penalty she would pay for living with a man to whom she was not married.

She would no longer exist as far as her parents and her family were concerned.

She would be ostracised from everything that was familiar.

She would lose everything she had known ever since she was a child.

Yet her love had been big enough to face that and to take her baby with her.

'That is love . . . that is *real* love!' Claudia thought. 'When absolutely nothing else in the world matters except the person who holds your heart.'

Slowly, she walked back to the bed.

As she got into it, she suddenly felt cold, and she shivered.

The dream was over and the party had ended!

Once again she was alone in the world with nothing but her memories.

*   *   *

Claudia awoke, knowing that she had cried herself to sleep.

She realised that, as the maid was pulling back the curtains, it was eight o'clock.

She remembered what she had decided last night after she had cried and cried into her pillow.

As the maid finished the curtains, she said:

"I have a headache, and I would be very grateful if you would have breakfast brought up here for me."

"I order it, *Señora*," the maid replied.

It was twenty minutes later that the breakfast came upstairs.

When it was put down beside her, Claudia said:

"Have His Royal Highness and my husband left the Palace yet?"

"I see them drive away, *Señora*, as I come up staircase."

"Would you please ask Her Royal Highness, Princess Louisa, to come and speak to me?"

The maid left the room.

Claudia had finished her breakfast by the time the Princess came bursting in.

"You are not ill?" she asked. "I was waiting for you in the Breakfast-Room."

"I have a . . . headache," Claudia replied, "and please . . . I want your help."

"My help?" Princess Louisa asked in surprise.

"I have had very bad news from London," Claudia said. "My Grandmother, whose illness nearly prevented me from sailing with my husband, has had a sudden relapse. I must therefore go to her at once."

"At once?" the Princess exclaimed.

"If I wait until to-morrow, it may be too late and she may be dead," Claudia explained.

"She has always been very kind to me, and I love her very much, so please . . . please, Your Royal Highness, help me to reach her as quickly as possible."

"Of course I will do that," Princess Louisa promised. "I will go downstairs now and tell the Secretary who sees to all Papa's travels and mine, when I go abroad. He is very efficient."

"I am so very grateful!" Claudia said.

The Princess left, and Claudia quickly got up.

She called the maid and asked her to get some other maids to help pack her clothes as quickly as possible.

By the time the Princess came back, there were three maids putting Claudia's clothes into the smart trunks which Lady Bressley had given her.

"Everything is arranged," Princess Louisa said, "and you have to leave in half-an-hour."

She paused before she added:

"The Secretary was surprised that you are travelling alone. He will send a Courier with you to the station to see that you have a compartment to yourself."

Claudia thought this was helpful, and she thanked her.

"I will come with you to the station," Princess Louisa said impulsively. "I must go and get my hat."

As soon as she had left the room, Claudia

119

went to the *secrétaire*, which stood near the window.

She put a piece of crested writing-paper down on the blotter, then she hesitated.

Finally, she wrote quickly:

The dream is ended, so I have gone home. I have told the Princess that my Grandmother, whose illness nearly prevented me from coming with you in the first place, is very much worse, and may die.

Claudia

She put the writing-paper into an envelope.

She was just about to seal it down, when she had a thought.

She went to the dressing-table and took out her hand-bag.

In it, unopened, was the envelope in which the Marquis told her he had put a cheque for 1,000 pounds.

On an impulse, she tore the cheque in two and enclosed it with her note in the envelope on which she wrote his name.

She sealed it.

When the Princess joined her a few minutes later, they went down the stairs together.

When they reached the hall, Claudia put the envelope addressed to the Marquis on a table.

She knew it would be given to him on his return.

One of the Royal carriages was waiting.

Behind it was a less grand vehicle in which two footmen were placing her luggage.

Claudia saw that the Courier who was accompanying her to the station was supervising the operation.

She and Princess Louisa got into the carriage.

"I shall miss you!" Princess Louisa said sadly. "I do wish you could have stayed longer."

"When you come to England, perhaps we will meet again," Claudia answered.

"I would love that," Princess Louisa said, "but from what Papa said to me at breakfast, I think he is now considering taking me to Hungary."

"Is there a Prince there who you might marry?" Claudia asked.

Princess Louisa nodded.

"He sounds rather exciting! Hungarians have the reputation of being marvellous horsemen, and very ardent lovers."

Claudia felt somehow shocked that Princess Louisa should say such things.

Then she told herself she was being very prudish.

At the same time, she did not wish to think about love at the moment.

As they drove to the station, she tried to listen to Princess Louisa, and at the same time have her last look at Seville.

It was a place she had never expected to see.

Yet, now she knew it would always remain in her memory.

She knew, too, that if nothing else, she would never forget that the Marquis had kissed her last night.

Everything at the Railway Station was arranged for her in the most Regal manner.

She and Princess Louisa were taken into the Royal Waiting-Room.

One of the walls was embellished with an enormous Coat-of-Arms surmounted by a crown.

They were offered coffee or wine.

They both chose coffee at that early hour of the morning.

"I shall miss you! I shall miss you!" Princess Louisa kept saying. "Oh, please, please, come back and stay another time! I am sure your husband will want to do so."

"I am sure he will," Claudia agreed soothingly.

When the train arrived, the Station-Master came to escort Claudia to the compartment which had been reserved for her.

To her delight, it was in a sleeping-car.

These were rare, even in the trains which

journeyed right across Europe.

The Station-Master informed her that she would have to change at Paris.

He had telegraphed through to say that a compartment must be reserved on the train which was to take her to Calais.

Claudia thanked him profusely.

Then she said to Princess Louisa in French, because she thought he would not understand:

"I do not think I have to tip the Station-Master, but what about the porters?"

"The Courier will see to all that," the Princess said.

"And . . . my fare?"

"The Marquis will pay for that," Princess Louisa said casually.

For a moment Claudia hesitated.

She wanted to pay for herself out of the ready money the Marquis had given her.

Then she told herself there might not be enough to get her to England.

Moreover, the Princess would think it strange that she did not wish to be beholden to her own husband.

The two girls kissed each other affectionately.

Claudia got into the carriage.

The conductor, having been told she was of importance, was waiting to take her to her sleeper.

Claudia, however, stood at the door as the

train moved off, waving to the Princess until she was out of sight.

Her compartment was in the centre of the sleeping-car, so that it was not over the wheels.

The conductor was only too willing to bring her anything she required.

When Claudia was finally alone, she sat at the window to have a last look at Seville.

She was also saying good-bye to the Marquis.

"I shall never see him again," she told herself. "But I will never, never forget him!"

She knew what she would never forget was the feeling of rapture when his lips had touched hers.

She'd had no idea it was possible to feel such sensations.

When she thought it over, she felt she should have guessed she was in love.

Every time she had seen him come into a room or speak to her, there had been a strange feeling in her breast that she had never known before.

It was love, and it was, she knew, the same feeling that her Mother had for Walter Wilton.

'That is the way I love him!' she thought as the train gathered speed. 'But it is not the way he loves me.'

The servants from the Palace had put newspapers into her carriage.

There was also a magazine that was published in Seville.

What she appreciated most was a large hamper.

She knew it would contain food which would last for most of the journey.

It meant that she would not have the expense of going to the restaurant-car, if there was one.

Or, as was more usual on foreign railways, to buy packaged meals quickly when they stopped at a station.

There might also be men who would try to get into conversations with her because she was unaccompanied.

'I am lucky, so very lucky,' she thought.

She might have had to return to England in steerage class in an Ocean Liner from Cadiz.

That was what she had thought she must do when Lady Bressley had been killed.

The day passed slowly because she could not help thinking of the Marquis.

She wondered what he would say when he got back to the Palace and found she had gone.

Perhaps, in a way, he would be quite glad to be rid of her.

She would no longer be a problem to him.

She went over and over every word he had said to her last night, remembering the intonation in his voice.

She could see the expression in his eyes when he told her he could not marry her.

She thrilled as she remembered the fire in them when he had kissed her.

"I love him! I love him!" she said over and over again.

The very wheels seemed to be repeating the words.

"I love him! I love him! Completely and endlessly!"

When she went to bed she cried again because she was now so far away from him.

* * *

Claudia arrived in Paris early the next morning.

It was a relief when the conductor informed her that there was an Official to escort her to the train bound for Calais, which would first take her slowly round Paris to the Gare du Nord.

A number of other people on the train were apparently changing to the same one as Claudia was.

She noticed a number of English people who looked at her curiously.

All she had to do was to thank the Official, who told her he was acting on behalf of the Station-Master, and tip the porters.

They had placed her luggage in the Guard's Van.

When the train was about to move off, she was locked into her reserved compartment.

The train reached Calais in the middle of the afternoon.

Now, for the first time, Claudia had to look after herself.

With difficulty she found a porter.

Only because she begged him in her good French to help her did he condescend to find her luggage.

She had no idea that because she seemed so young the porter had decided to befriend her.

Without her suggesting it, he engaged a cabin on the steamship that was to carry her to Dover.

It was something she had not thought of doing.

When she looked at the rest of the passengers, however, she was grateful to be alone.

She tipped the porter generously.

He did not mind that she gave him English money.

She thought that if she had any sense, she would have changed some in Paris.

But it had not occurred to her.

Having been spoiled on the first part of her journey, she told herself she should not complain now.

* * *

In the train from Dover to London, Claudia found herself in a Second Class carriage.

It was filled with people who were either noisy, or eating.

The Steward on the steamship had brought her a few sandwiches.

She had, of course, long ago consumed the contents of the hamper.

There had also been a choice of tea or coffee to drink.

Now she felt hungry, but her fellow passengers did not offer her any of their large sausages and fat rolls.

They were guzzling themselves, stopping only to wash the food down by drinking out of a bottle.

It was a relief to reach London, although it was eleven o'clock in the evening.

Once again, Claudia had great difficulty in finding a porter.

Then, only because she was so well dressed, the driver of a Hackney Carriage agreed to take her.

The Cabby in a surly voice said he was going home.

Claudia remembered while she was in the train that she would have to get the key to the house in Chelsea from Mr. Prior, Lady Bressley's Secretary.

What was more, she realised she had a disagreeable task ahead of her.

Unless the Courier who had broken his leg in the accident had informed the household what had happened, she would have to break the news of Lady Bressley's death.

The Hackney Carriage drew up outside the large house in Grosvenor Square.

The coachman, however, made no attempt to climb down from his box.

Claudia got out and rang the bell.

She rang and rang.

Then she raised the knocker again and again, but there was no answer.

She thought despairingly that she might have to spend the night on the doorstep.

At last, however, to her relief, there was the sound of bolts being drawn back, and the door opened.

A sleepy-eyed footman, half-dressed, asked in a hostile voice:

"Wot d'yer want?"

"I want to speak to Mr. Prior," Claudia said.

The footman stared at her.

Then, realising that she seemed to be someone of importance, he opened the door a little wider.

"Oi thinks Mister Prior might've gorn t' bed, Ma'am," he said, "but Oi'll tell 'im yer wants 'im."

"Yes, please do that," Claudia said.

The footman disappeared.

Claudia was extremely relieved when a few minutes later Mr. Prior, fully-dressed, appeared.

"Miss Coventry!" he exclaimed in astonishment when he saw who was waiting. "I was not expecting you, least of all at this hour of the night! Is Her Ladyship with you?"

"I have a lot to tell you, Mr. Prior," Claudia said, "and please, would it be possible for me to stay here for to-night? I do not think the Cabby who brought me here will wait while I am talking to you."

She had only just thought of the idea of staying in Grosvenor Square.

She was certain that Mr. Prior would want to know every detail concerning Lady Bressley's death.

Her luggage was brought in, and she paid the Cabby, who gruffly acknowledged the tip she gave him.

Mr. Prior then took Claudia into a small Sitting-Room which opened off the hall.

"Is there anything I can get you?" he asked. "Something to eat or drink?"

"I am sure it is too much trouble," Claudia said, "but I have had nothing to eat since I left the steamship that brought me across the Channel."

Mr. Prior looked at her in amazement.

Then he hurried away to give a footman the order to wake the cook.

"I am sorry to be such a nuisance," Claudia said apologetically, "but I am very tired, and I have to tell you why I am here."

Mr. Prior sat down in a chair.

"What has happened, Miss Coventry?" he asked.

"I regret to have to inform you that Lady Bressley is dead," Claudia replied.

When she saw the expression of shock on his face, she knew it was the last thing he had expected her to say.

She suspected he had been thinking that she had been sent back in disgrace, or, that for some other reason, Lady Bressley had dispensed with her.

"I can't believe it!" Mr. Prior said.

Claudia told him exactly what had happened.

He asked her a great number of questions.

She told him how the Courier had been injured in the accident, and how an Englishman had befriended her and taken her with him to Seville, from where she had caught a train home.

She was glad when Mr. Prior's cross-examination ended.

An omelette was produced, which being so hungry, she much enjoyed.

Then a chambermaid, who had dressed quickly, took her upstairs to the bedroom she had occupied before she and Lady Bressley had left for Spain.

It seemed incredible that so much had happened since she had last slept there.

She was very tired, and went to sleep without crying.

* * *

Everything seemed very different the next morning.

Claudia was sent in Lady Bressley's carriage to the house in Chelsea.

She thanked Mr. Prior, learning that he had sent a woman to clean it after she had left.

Then he asked:

"You are not going to live there by yourself, Miss Coventry?"

"I have not yet decided what I shall do," Claudia replied. "As you doubtless know, my parents are dead and Lady Bressley had promised she would look after me."

Mr. Prior shook his head.

"It is very sad," he said. "I find it hard to believe that Her Ladyship will never be with us again."

The footman, who escorted her to the little house, carried in the luggage and set it down in the hall.

"Would y' like me to take it upstairs, Miss?" he enquired.

"That would be very kind," Claudia answered.

She knew she would not be able to manage the trunks by herself.

She tipped him before he left.

The carriage drove away.

Claudia shut the door, and she told herself she had to be practical and count how much money she had before she spent any more.

The payment for the main part of her journey had been left to the Marquis.

But she found her fares on the ship, and train to London, plus tips, had left her with only twenty pounds of ready money with which to face the future.

"I will go to the Bank and see if there is anything in . . . Walter Wilton's account," she told herself.

She could remember her Mother saying, however, that she hoped he would soon have a benefit.

She had also added:

"I find it embarrassing to keep giving orders to the Butcher when I cannot pay him."

Knowing there was nothing in the house to eat, Claudia thought she must go to the shops.

Then she saw her hamper standing on the kitchen table.

When she opened it, she found that Mr. Prior had been more thoughtful than she had expected him to be.

The hamper had been filled again, and besides food there was a tin of coffee beans.

"Everyone is so . . . kind to me," she told herself.

At the same time, she knew there was only one person she wanted to think of her.

That was the Marquis.

Because she knew she had to put him out of her mind, she went upstairs.

As she entered her Mother's bedroom, the scent of white violets was there.

Quite suddenly she felt like a child who had been hurt and wanted comforting.

She took off her hat and travelling cloak and went down on her knees beside her Mother's bed.

"Help me . . . Mama . . . help me," she begged. "I do not know . . . what to . . . do and I keep . . . wishing that I had . . . not run away . . . but it would have been . . . wrong to stay . . . with him . . . so help me . . . now to forget . . . him and decide . . . whether I . . . live . . . here or . . . try and go to my . . . Father."

She found it hard to say the last words.

The Earl of Strathniven seemed a very frightening, strange old man from whom her Mother had run away.

Why should he care about her?

He had made no effort to see her for seventeen years after she had been taken from his Castle.

Then she felt as if her Mother were beside her.

She was smiling and Claudia was sure her hand gently touched her forehead.

The tears came into Claudia's eyes, but they were tears of happiness.

She was not alone. Her Mother was still with her.

* * *

The house had been well cleaned, thanks to Mr. Prior.

When Claudia went downstairs again, she wondered if she should get in touch with Kitty.

Then she told herself that was something she could not afford.

She had to be careful with every penny until she could find some way of earning money.

She started to itemize her talents, but they were not very saleable.

She could sew, but so could most other women.

She could speak French, but who would want to employ her when she was so young?

Although she was well read, she was quite certain that no-one would engage her as a Governess. Without being conceited, she knew that she was too pretty to be considered for the position.

'I will have to go to my Father,' she thought despairingly.

If he rejected her—what then?

The question was inescapably there, however much she tried to evade it.

She went into the rooms, one after another.

Because they were clean and tidy, there was nothing for her to do.

"To-morrow morning I will go to the Bank," she decided.

She knew the food which had been put in the hamper would not last for ever.

She would have to go to the shops.

She had to be very careful what she bought, otherwise she would have to sell her Mother's jewellery.

Then there would be nothing more except for the house itself.

She had the feeling that it would not fetch very much even with its contents.

Once again she went to Walter Wilton's desk.

She had been through it once.

"I had better do so again," she said aloud, "just in case there is something I have overlooked."

Unexpectedly there was a knock on the door.

For a moment she thought she must have imagined it.

Then it came again.

Reluctantly, because she was afraid it would be something unpleasant, she moved from the Sitting-Room into the small hall.

She had bolted the door because she had not expected to be going out again.

Slowly she drew back the bolt.

Then, as she opened the door, she gasped.

It was the Marquis who stood there.

chapter seven

FOR a moment Claudia could not believe it was true, and she just stared at him.

The Marquis walked in through the doorway, pushed the door shut behind him, and flung his top-hat down on a chair.

Then—and Claudia did not know whether he moved or she did—she was in his arms.

He was kissing her passionately, fiercely, almost brutally.

She melted against him as he swept her into the Heaven where he had taken her when he kissed her before.

This time it was far more vivid, far more thrilling, far more rapturous than anything she had ever known.

The Marquis went on kissing her until they were both breathless.

Then, suddenly aware that they were standing in the hall, he pulled her through the open doorway of the Sitting-Room.

He did not take his arms from her, and it was impossible for her to speak.

She knew only that she was aware of nothing except him.

He blazed like a brilliant light which enveloped her completely.

The Marquis pushed the Sitting-Room door shut, then he was kissing her again.

Only when she gave a little murmur because he was so overwhelming did he raise his head.

Claudia buried her face against his shoulder, and he said in a voice she hardly recognised:

"My Darling! My sweet! Are you all right? When I found I had lost you, I thought I should go mad!"

It was impossible for Claudia to answer him, and he went on:

"Forgive me! You have to forgive me! How could I have been such a fool as to think I could live without you?"

He put his fingers under her chin, and turned her face up to his.

"You are mine!" he said fiercely. "And we are being married this evening."

Claudia could hardly take in what he was saying.

Yet somehow she managed to question: "Mar-ried?"

"Yes, married!" the Marquis said firmly. "And there will be no argument about it!"

He kissed her violently, as if he were fighting his relations who would question the wisdom of such a marriage.

Claudia wanted to tell him the truth about who she was.

It was, however, impossible for her to speak when his lips were holding hers captive.

At last she was free and she said:

"Listen . . . please listen to . . . me!"

"All I can think about is that I have found you!" he insisted. "How could you do anything so utterly cruel as to go off like that, knowing it would make me frantic?"

"I . . . I had to . . . go," Claudia murmured.

"It was all my fault," the Marquis admitted, "but it is something which will never happen again."

His lips sought hers, but she tried to prevent him from kissing her.

"There is something I want . . ." she began.

At that moment the door opened.

They instinctively moved apart as one of the Marquis's servants said:

" 'Scuse me, M'Lord, but there's a Gent'man 'ere askin' to see th' Lady o' th' 'Ouse."

Before the Marquis could reply, a man

pushed past the servant and came into the room.

He was an impressive figure in a kilt and carrying his bonnet in his hand.

His hair was nearly white, and he had a small beard.

"Ah'm asking," he said in a broad Scottish accent, "tae speak wi' Lady—"

He stopped suddenly and looked at Claudia.

"Ah ken who ye are, M'Lady, wi'out ye tellin' me," he said. "Ye're verry much like your Mother."

Claudia, with an effort, moved towards him.

But before she could reach him, the Marquis intervened:

"Who are you?" he demanded. "And why are you here?"

The Scotsman looked at him as if he did not realise until that moment that he was in the room.

"M' name, Sir," he said, "is Talbot McNiven. Ah've come here on the orders o' ma Chieftain, tae bring Her Ladyship back tae Scotland."

"Your Chieftain?" the Marquis exclaimed. "And who is he?"

Claudia realised he was being somewhat hostile.

He thought the man was an interloper, and perhaps in some way attached to her.

"Ma Chieftain," Talbot McNiven said in a dignified manner, "is the Earl o' Strathniven."

"The Earl of Strathniven?" the Marquis repeated. "I have shot on his moors when I was staying at Brorer Castle."

The Scotsman smiled.

"His Grace has some fine moorlands himself," he said, "and an excellent salmon river."

"I agree," the Marquis said, "but I cannot understand why you are here."

It was then that Claudia intervened.

She had stood bewildered while the two men were talking.

"I was . . . going to . . . tell you," she said, "I was . . . trying to . . . tell you."

"Tell me—what?" the Marquis enquired.

"Please . . . could I speak to you . . . alone?" Claudia said frantically.

She was afraid that what she was about to say would somehow upset him.

She could not bear that it should happen with a stranger in the room.

As if the Marquis understood, he said:

"Of course."

Turning to Talbot McNiven, he said:

"If you would make yourself comfortable here, I will ask my servant to get you some refreshment while I have a private conversation with the Lady you have apparently come to see."

" 'Courrse, o'courrse, Sir," Talbot McNiven agreed.

The Marquis took Claudia by the hand and drew her to the door.

In the hall the Marquis's servant was standing by the open front-door.

"See if you can find tea or coffee, or anything to drink for the Gentleman in the Sitting-Room," the Marquis ordered.

"Very good, M'Lord," the man replied.

The Marquis looked down at Claudia.

"Where shall we go?" he asked.

She was finding it hard to speak, so she just pulled him by the hand up the stairs.

She took him into the Drawing-Room, which was a pretty room.

It seemed to her, however, small and insignificant after the huge *Salons* in the Palace.

The Marquis did not even look round.

He just shut the door behind him, and putting his arms around Claudia, he said:

"Now, what is all this about? Who is this man and what does he want with you? What can you possibly have to do with the Earl of Strathniven?"

Claudia drew a deep breath.

"H-he is . . . my F-Father," she answered.

The Marquis stared at her.

Taking his arms from her, he asked:

"What are you saying? I do not understand!"

"My Mother was married to . . . the Viscount Niven . . . but she . . . ran away . . . from

him . . . when I was only a . . . year old,"
Claudia said, "and . . . none of the . . . family
ever . . . spoke to . . . her again."

"Your Mother ran away—with Walter
Wilton?" the Marquis asked as if he were
trying to get it straight in his own mind.

Claudia nodded.

"I was . . . going to . . . tell you," she murmured. "I was just . . . going to . . . tell you."

"And who was your Mother before she
married?" the Marquis asked.

"She was the daughter of the Earl of
Porthcarion."

"I know the present Earl," the Marquis said,
"and I think he must be your uncle, but you let
me think when we first talked at the Hotel, and
again at the Palace, that you were the daughter
of Walter Wilton!"

"If you had . . . known who I . . . really was
you would . . . never have asked me to help
you in such a way, nor would you have
thought I could carry it off. As it was, since I
had no money after Lady Bressley was killed,
it seemed . . . foolish not to . . . accept your . . .
suggestion that I act the part of . . . your
wife. It . . . it was . . . wrong of me, but . . .
I suppose . . . because of . . . the accident . . . I
was not thinking clearly."

"And if you had refused me," the Marquis
said, "I would never have known that I loved

you as I have never loved anyone before."

"Please . . . please forgive . . . me for . . . deceiving you," Claudia begged, "but . . . when you . . . asked me to . . . live with . . . you as . . . Mama lived with . . . Walter Wilton I . . . knew I could . . . not do so. It would . . . be wrong."

"Why did you think it would be wrong?" the Marquis asked gently.

The colour surged into Claudia's face, and she looked away from him.

When she did not reply, he said:

"You thought I did not love you enough. That was what was wrong?"

Claudia nodded.

"You were right," he said unexpectedly. "Of course you were right! I did not realise at that moment that I loved you so that nothing in the whole world mattered except that I could not lose you."

He gave a little smile before he added:

"I was determined not to be like Christopher Columbus and lose everything I had discovered!"

"And so . . . so you . . . followed me," Claudia said. "How did you . . . get here so . . . quickly?"

"I caught the Midnight Express to Ostend," the Marquis said, "and I reached Tilbury very late last night."

"H-how did you . . . find out . . . where I . . . lived?"

"I went first to my house in Park Lane," the Marquis replied, "and I told my Secretary to get a Special Marriage Licence. I also sent a groom to the country to tell my Chaplain to be ready to marry us in my Private Chapel as soon as we arrived."

"But . . . how could you have . . . known where . . . I would be?"

The Marquis smiled again.

"I had all night on the train to worry about it—frantic in case something terrible should happen to you, or perhaps some man insult you. Then I remembered that you had been, as I assumed, employed by Lady Bressley."

"So you went to her house in Grosvenor Square."

"As soon as I had made all the arrangements for our marriage," the Marquis said, "I went there expecting to find you. It was her Secretary who told me that you had already come here."

"It all sounds so easy!" Claudia exclaimed. "But . . . I thought . . . I believed . . . that I would . . . never see . . . you again."

The Marquis put his arms around her.

"How could I lose you?" he asked.

Claudia put both hands against his chest to prevent him from drawing her too close to him.

"Listen to me . . . please listen," she said. "Lady Bressley told me that in Scotland they were . . . horrified when . . . Mama ran . . . away and left my . . . F-Father. If you marry me . . . even though I am my . . . Mother's daughter . . . they will still talk . . . and perhaps it might . . . hurt you."

The Marquis gave a laugh, and it was a very happy sound.

"My precious Darling," he said. "Only you could be thinking of me instead of yourself. If the Scots talk, let them! I was prepared to marry you if you were the daughter of a crossing-sweeper, and face any anger or unpleasantness from the whole world rather than lose you."

He drew in his breath.

"But," he went on, "as the daughter of the Earl of Strathniven, my family will be delighted to accept you as my wife and, if there are any criticisms, they will certainly not make them to me."

"Then . . . I can . . . marry you?" Claudia asked. "I really can?"

"It is something you are going to do," the Marquis said in a deep voice. "My Darling, how could you have made me suffer as I have these last twenty-four hours, with no-one to blame but myself!"

Claudia hid her face against his neck.

"The truth . . . was," she said in a whisper, "that I . . . ran away because . . . I loved

146

you . . . so much . . . that I . . . wanted to . . . agree to what you suggested."

"It is something I deeply regret suggesting," the Marquis said as if he were angry with himself. "You are perfect and only someone utterly unprincipled would spoil you."

"I shall never . . . never forget," Claudia said still in a very low voice, "that now you . . . wanted to marry me . . . even though you thought I was Walter Wilton's daughter."

"I understand so well now," the Marquis said, "why you are as you are. You bewildered and at the same time intrigued me, because you were so innocent, so unspoiled, and yet so exquisitely beautiful that wherever you were in the world there would have been men kneeling at your feet."

Claudia made a little murmur, and the Marquis continued:

"I suppose what I ought to do is to let you, as your real Father's daughter, meet people in the Social World and other men, in case you find someone you love more than me."

Claudia gave a little cry.

"No, no . . . of course not! How could you . . . suggest such . . . a thing!"

"I can assure you," the Marquis said as he smiled, "it is something I have no intention of putting into practice. You are mine, mine completely and absolutely. I would no more lose you, my precious, than lose my own life!"

Then he was kissing her again, kissing her so that she felt that she was completely a part of him and nothing could divide them.

*   *   *

It seemed a long time before Claudia said:

"We have forgotten Mr. McNiven."

"Yes, of course," the Marquis agreed as if he had forgotten him too. "We will send him back to your Father to tell him that when our honeymoon is over we will come to Scotland to meet him. He might even give us an invitation to stay during the grouse season!"

Claudia laughed.

"That may be something I can give you. You already possess everything else."

"It is something quite different that I want from you," the Marquis said softly.

They looked into each other's eyes.

Then, as if he pulled himself to attention, he said:

"Come along, we have a great deal to do. I suggest, my Darling, that you put on your hat and I will send the servants to take your luggage, which I suspect is as yet unpacked, downstairs."

"It is in the next room," Claudia said.

The Marquis took her hand, and they walked down the stairs, side by side.

The front-door was open and Claudia saw

the sunshine streaming in in a golden haze.

Only then did she know that she was once again moving in a wonderful dream.

The darkness and misery which had encompassed her since she left Seville had gone for ever.

* * *

After an early luncheon at the large house in Park Lane, they set off for the country.

The Marquis was driving a team of four chestnuts, which he told Claudia were a new acquisition.

"When I first saw . . . you driving your team," she told him, "I thought what a . . . brilliant driver you were and it . . . fascinated me."

"I intend to fascinate you in a great many ways," the Marquis replied, "and you must tell me what they are as you discover them."

Claudia gave a little laugh.

"I am . . . afraid that will make you more . . . conceited than you are . . . already!" she said teasingly.

"I was certainly not conceited last night," the Marquis replied, "when I boarded the Express in Seville. I lay awake, terrified in case you were in danger and I was not there to protect you."

"I was . . . so . . . unhappy," Claudia murmured, "when I arrived . . . here this morning in an empty house . . . and I was afraid because I . . . had so little money."

"That was another thing that frightened me," the Marquis said. "How could you have torn up my cheque? How did you think you could manage without it?"

"I . . . I thought," Claudia said a little shyly, "that I had not . . . done what . . . you wanted."

"You earned that money a thousand times over," the Marquis said. "No-one could have acted better than you did at the Palace, although of course I realise now that you were not acting. You were just being yourself and behaving as your Mother would have done."

"That is . . . true," Claudia said. "Mama was very insistent that I should always behave like a Lady."

"I cannot believe you needed much teaching," the Marquis said a little dryly.

Then he added softly:

"But I have a great many other things to teach you, my Darling, and the most important subject is Love!"

Claudia blushed, then she pressed her cheek against his arm.

It was an action which brought the fire to his eyes.

Instinctively, he drove his team a little faster.

They reached the Marquis's house in Hertfordshire in the record time of two-and-a-half hours.

As they turned into the great gold-tipped wrought-iron gates, Claudia looked ahead and saw one of the most beautiful houses she had ever imagined.

It was very large and the sunshine was sparkling on its windows.

The surrounding gardens were a blaze of colour, and it seemed to welcome her in a way she could not put into words.

As if the Marquis understood what she was thinking, he said gently:

"This is your home now, my Darling, but because I want you to myself, and I cannot allow you to be spoiled by the Social World, we will spend more time here than anywhere else."

"I have always wanted to live in the country," Claudia said. "When we used to go somewhere quiet for a holiday, I always thought it was more exciting than living in London."

"That is what we will find," the Marquis said confidently.

They drew up outside the front-door.

Two footmen wearing the Marquis's livery were rolling down a red carpet as the chaise came into view.

The Marquis and Claudia stepped out of the

chaise and walked up the steps together into an enormous hall.

"Welcome back, M'Lord!" the Butler said, bowing respectfully.

"Thank you, Dudley," the Marquis replied. "I hope the instructions I sent down this morning have all been carried out."

"They have indeed, M'Lord, and may I, on behalf of myself and the staff, wish Your Lordship and Her Ladyship every happiness."

The Marquis introduced Claudia to the Butler, who took her upstairs to the House-keeper.

Their luggage had left for the country before they had, and was already unpacked.

Her bedroom, Claudia learned, had been occupied by the Marquis's Mother.

The Housekeeper, who had been there for thirty years, asked:

"What will Your Ladyship wear for the wedding?"

"I . . . I had not . . . thought," Claudia answered.

Because she was longing to go back downstairs to be with the Marquis, she hastily washed her hands.

Then she left everything to the Housekeeper.

They had tea in the Drawing-Room, which was so lovely that she could hardly believe it was to be her home.

Then the Marquis took her upstairs.

"We are having a very quiet wedding, my precious," he said, "but it is something I want you to remember all our lives."

"How could I ever . . . forget it when I am . . . marrying you?" Claudia answered.

"That is what I am saying in my heart," the Marquis replied. "At the same time, you must look beautiful, and that is why you will find in your room the bridal veil that has been worn by every Marchioness for the last two-hundred years. There is also a diamond tiara which my Mother wore when she married my Father."

He saw the question in Claudia's eyes and knew what she was asking him without words.

"Theirs was not an arranged marriage," he said. "They fell in love with each other quite naturally, for my Mother's parents lived only three miles from here."

Claudia laughed.

"Then it is not surprising that they fell in love."

"They were very happy," the Marquis assured her, "and that is what we will be—although I fell in love with you in a Spanish Hotel, when I thought I was dreaming or that you were just a part of my imagination."

As he finished speaking they had reached her bedroom door.

He lifted her hand to his lips and said gently:

"Do not keep me waiting. I am a very impatient Bridegroom."

Claudia was laughing as she entered her bedroom and shut the door.

The Housekeeper was already there.

She had spread out a beautiful white gown on the bed.

Lady Bressley had bought it for Claudia, but she had never even put it on.

It had a bustle of chiffon and lace.

Above the tiny waist, the bodice was covered with diamanté and pearls.

Claudia felt that perhaps Lady Bressley had had a premonition that it was what she would need as a wedding-gown.

When she was dressed, the veil was flowing over her gown to the floor.

The sparkling diamond tiara which held it in place made her look, she told herself, like a Fairy Princess.

She knew the Marquis would be waiting for her in the hall.

A footman had brought her the message at the same time that he carried in a bouquet of white orchids and lilies-of-the-valley.

Claudia went down the wide staircase, with its carved and gilded balustrade.

She saw the Marquis and realised he was looking as smart as she was.

The breast of his cut-away coat was covered in decorations, and he wore the Order of the

Garter across one shoulder.

As she joined him, they just looked at each other, there was no need for words.

She saw the love in his eyes.

She knew that no-one could be luckier than she was at that moment.

It was a long walk to the Chapel, which had been built at the back of the house when it had been renovated by the Adam brothers in 1750.

As they reached the door, Claudia could hear the organ softly playing.

There was no-one inside except for the Chaplain dressed in his white vestments, and the Marquis's Secretary, who was to be their witness.

The Service was very simple.

But Claudia felt sure her Mother was near her and that the angels were singing.

When the Marquis had put the ring on her finger, they both knelt for the blessing.

She knew then that God had blessed her and she could never express her gratitude in words.

"Please," she prayed, "let my husband . . . love me for ever. Let me . . . help him to bring . . . happiness to . . . other people . . . and please . . . God, let me give him . . . sons as . . . wonderful as . . . he is."

It was a prayer that came from the very depths of her heart.

Then the organ was playing the Wedding March and the Marquis escorted her from the Chapel.

They received the congratulations of the staff before they went upstairs to take off their wedding garments.

"I have arranged," the Marquis said, "that we will have supper alone in your *Boudoir*. So for now, just put on something comfortable, which I am sure will be waiting for you."

His idea of "something comfortable" was a very attractive négligée that had been in one of her trunks.

She had never worn it before.

It covered her diaphanous nightgown, but she felt very shy.

Her hair was still arranged as it had been for the wedding.

Otherwise, she told herself, she was ready for bed.

She went into the *Boudoir*, and the Marquis was waiting for her.

He was wearing the same dark robe he had worn when he had come to her bedroom in the Palace.

Their supper was laid on the table, but there were no servants in attendance.

"I am going to serve you," the Marquis said, "and kiss you, my Darling, between every course."

Claudia gave a little cry of delight.

"That is . . . all I . . . want," she said, "to be . . . alone with . . . you."

"By a strange coincidence," the Marquis replied, "that is what I want, too."

He kissed her, and knowing she wanted him to go on kissing her, he said:

"If you excite me, my Darling, we will go to bed hungry. Sit down at the table. We have done a lot to-day, and I have to look after you and make sure you take care of yourself."

Claudia laughed.

"That is what I should be . . . saying to you . . . and it is . . . something I shall . . . always do in the . . . future."

Claudia had no idea what they ate.

She knew only that because the Marquis was with her, it tasted like ambrosia.

They toasted each other with champagne, but she could see only the sparkle in the Marquis's eyes and she knew how much she excited him.

When supper was finished, he took her into the bedroom.

The curtains were drawn and there were only two candles flickering by those which hung from a golden corola over the bed.

The Marquis took the pins from Claudia's hair, and it fell over her shoulders nearly to her waist.

"That was how you looked," he said softly, "when I came to your room in the Palace. I can never tell you what an agony it was not to touch you, and to keep my promise that I would not embarrass you."

"I did . . . not know . . . then," Claudia whispered, "how wonderful a . . . kiss could . . . be."

"It was a kiss which I had never given or received before," the Marquis said. "When I left you, I cursed myself for making a promise I had to keep."

He gave a short laugh.

"Now there are no promises, and I can tell you how much I love you!"

They looked into each other's eyes.

Then, picking Claudia up in his arms, he carried her to the bed.

He put her down gently with her head resting against the pillow.

As he joined her, Claudia felt a wild excitement sweep through her.

She knew now that this was what she had been longing for but what she had thought she would never find.

"I . . . love . . . you," she whispered, "I love you . . . so . . . much that I . . . have no . . . words in which to express what . . . I feel."

"There is no need for words," the Marquis said in a deep voice.

His lips were seeking hers, his hand was touching her body, and she knew he was right.

She was thrilled with an ecstasy that was

beyond anything she had ever known or imagined.

It swept her up into the sky.

She knew this was Love.

The real love for which she had longed and was the treasure that everybody seeks and hopes one day to find.

She knew what she and the Marquis had found was something that would never change.

It would be theirs, now and for the rest of their lives.

"I adore and worship you, my beautiful wife!" the Marquis was saying. "I feel as if I have climbed the Himalayas, and plunged into the ocean to find you. You are mine! Mine! And never again will I lose you!"

Then he made her his, and they were no longer two people, but one.

"I . . . love you," she whispered.

"I adore and worship you," the Marquis said, "my Precious, my Darling, my perfect little wife."

She knew that never again would it be just a dream, but a love that would last for all Eternity.

ABOUT THE AUTHOR

BARBARA CARTLAND, the world's most famous romantic novelist, who is also an historian, playwright, lecturer, political speaker and television personality, has now written over 596 books and sold over six hundred and twenty million copies all over the world.

She has also had many historical works published and has written four autobiographies as well as the biographies of her mother and that of her brother, Ronald Cartland, who was the first Member of Parliament to be killed in the last war. This book has a preface by Sir Winston Churchill and has just been republished with an introduction by Sir Arthur Bryant.

Love at the Helm, a novel written with the help and inspiration of the late Earl Mountbatten of Burma, Great Uncle of His Royal Highness, The Prince of Wales, is being sold for the Mountbatten Memorial Trust.

She has broken the world record for the last sixteen years by writing an average of twenty-three books a year. In the *Guinness Book of World Records* she is listed as the world's top-selling author.

Miss Cartland in 1987 sang an Album of Love Songs with the Royal Philharmonic Orchestra.

In private life Barbara Cartland, who is a Dame of the Order of St. John of Jerusalem and Chairman of the St. John Council in Hertfordshire, has fought for better conditions and salaries for Midwives and Nurses.

She championed the cause for the Elderly in 1956, invoking a Government Enquiry into the "Housing Condition of Old People."

In 1962 she had the Law of England changed so that Local Authorities had to provide camps for their own Gypsies. This has meant that since then thousands and thousands of Gypsy children have been able to go to School, which they had never been able to do in the past, as their caravans were moved every twenty-four hours by the Police.

There are now fifteen camps in Hertfordshire and Barbara Cartland has her own Romany

Gypsy Camp called "Barbaraville" by the Gypsies.

Her designs "Decorating with Love" are being sold all over the U.S.A. and the National Home Fashions League made her, in 1981, "Woman of Achievement."

She is unique in that she was one and two in the Dalton list of Best Sellers, and one week had four books in the top twenty.

Barbara Cartland's book *Getting Older, Growing Younger* has been published in Great Britain and the U.S.A. and her fifth cookery book, *The Romance of Food*, is now being used by the House of Commons.

In 1984 she received at Kennedy Airport America's Bishop Wright Air Industry Award for her contribution to the development of aviation. In 1931 she and two R.A.F. Officers thought of, and carried, the first aeroplane-towed glider airmail.

During the War she was Chief Lady Welfare Officer in Bedfordshire, looking after 20,000 Servicemen and -women. She thought of having a pool of Wedding Dresses at the War Office so a Service Bride could hire a gown for the day.

She bought 1,000 gowns without coupons for the A.T.S., the W.A.A.F.'s and the W.R.E.N.S. In 1945 Barbara Cartland received the Certificate of Merit from Eastern Command.

In 1964 Barbara Cartland founded the

National Association for Health of which she is the President, as a front for all the Health Stores and for any product made as alternative medicine.

This is now a £65 million turnover a year, with one-third going in export.

In January 1968 she received *La Médeille de Vermeil de la Ville de Paris*. This is the highest award to be given in France by the City of Paris. She has sold 30 million books in France.

In March 1988 Barbara Cartland was asked by the Indian Government to open their Health Resort outside Delhi. This is almost the largest Health Resort in the world.

Barbara Cartland was received with great enthusiasm by her fans, who feted her at a reception in the City, and she received the gift of an embossed plate from the Government.

Barbara Cartland was made a Dame of the Order of the British Empire in the 1991 New Year's Honours List by Her Majesty, The Queen, for her contribution to Literature and also for her years of work for the community.

Dame Barbara has now written 596 books, the greatest number by a British author, passing the 564 books written by John Creasey.

AWARDS

1945   Received Certificate of Merit, Eastern Command, for being Welfare Officer to 5,000 troops in Bedfordshire.

1953   Made a Commander of the Order of St. John of Jerusalem. Invested by H.R.H. The Duke of Gloucester at Buckingham Palace.

1972   Invested as Dame of Grace of the Order of St. John in London by The Lord Prior, Lord Cacia.

1981   Received "Achiever of the Year" from the National Home Furnishing Association in Colorado Springs, U.S.A., for her designs for wallpaper and fabrics.

1984   Received Bishop Wright Air Industry Award at Kennedy Airport, for inventing the aeroplane-towed Glider.

1988   Received from Monsieur Chirac, The Prime Minister, The Gold Medal of the City of Paris, at the Hotel de la Ville, Paris, for selling 25 million books and giving a lot of employment.

1991   Invested as Dame of the Order of The British Empire, by H.M. The Queen at Buckingham Palace for her contribution to Literature.